Cattle & Sheep & Boats

Other Titles by Geoffrey Lewis:

The D.I. David Russell Crime Novels:
Cycle	978-0-9545624-3-4
Flashback	978-0-9545624-0-3
Strangers	978-0-9545624-1-0
Winter's Tale	978-0-9545624-2-7
Gameboy	978-0-9564536-5-5

The Michael Baker Canal Trilogy:
A Boy Off The Bank	978-0-9545624-6-5
A Girl At The Tiller	978-0-9545624-7-2
The New Number One	978-0-9545624-8-9

The Jess Carter Children's Canal Stories:
Jess Carter & The Oil Boat	978-0-9564536-1-7
Jess Carter & The Bolinder	978-0-9564536-2-4

Other Canal Stories:
Starlight	978-0-9545624-5-8

And

Thunderchild	978-0-9551900-6-3

Being the first part of the Lord of the Storm fantasy
trilogy, published 2010.

Also:

L-Plate Boating (with Tom McManus)
978-0-9564536-0-0

All of these books can be obtained from our website –
and we do not charge for postage in the UK!
www.sgmpublishing.co.uk

Cattle & Sheep & Boats

Geoffrey Lewis

ISBN 978-0-9564536-3-1

First Published in Great Britain in 2012 by

SGM Publishing
47 Silicon Court, Shenley Lodge,
Milton Keynes MK5 7DJ
www.sgmpublishing.co.uk

ABOUT THE AUTHOR:

Geoffrey Lewis was born in Oxford, in 1947. Educated at the City's High School, and Hatfield University (then a polytechnic), he has since followed a varied career, including spells as a research chemist, security guard and professional photographer. After many years in the motor trade, and eight years as the owner and captain of a canal-based passenger boat, he is now semi-retired and concentrating upon writing.

After a childhood spent close to the Oxford Canal, his love of the waterways led him to live aboard a narrowboat on the Grand Union Canal for sixteen years. Now back on dry land, he lives in Milton Keynes, not far from the canal, and recently took on the duties of Captain on the historic pair *Nutfield* and *Raymond* which are to be seen at many waterways events through year.

Photographer, bell-ringer, real ale drinker and American car enthusiast, he is currently engaged upon a number of new writing projects, including a children's fantasy adventure trilogy after the style of Tolkein, of which *Thunderchild* is the first volume; and of course more stories set in the working days of England's canals!

A CAST OF CHARACTERS!

The people who populate this book, at least to begin with, are those from *The New Number One,* the last book of my 'Michael Baker' trilogy. I suspect many of you will have read those books, but I think it might be useful if I remind you of who they all are, and how they fit together.

You will meet many new characters in this book – but they will fit in as my story progresses! What follows here is a quick explanation of the central families as they were in August 1957, and how they all inter-relate. On the boats, people and families were often intertwined in quite complex ways – 'a bit of relation' was a common way of describing someone who was connected with you in some slightly distant fashion that would have otherwise taken a lot of explanation!

I hope you will remember the names that follow with affection and sympathy from the other books:

Michael Henry Baker: 'Mikey', 28 years old, the 'boy off the bank' who was 'adopted' by old Alby Baker (Boatman, now deceased) after running away from home in 1940. Previously known as Michael Thompson.

Harriet Baker: 27, Michael's wife, daughter of Henry and Suey Caplin (Boaters)

Caroline Baker: 'Carrie', 20, born Caroline Martin, 'adopted' into the Baker family after the death of her parents in a boating accident.

Albert Baker: 'Alby', 7, son of Michael and Harriet.
Susan Baker: 'Susie', 5, daughter of Michael and Harriet.
Frederick Baker: 'Freddie', 2, their second son.

Samuel Caplin: 'Sam', 23, brother to Harriet.
Virginia Caplin: 'Ginny', 23, his wife, and sister to Michael.

William Hanney: 'Bill', 61, ex-Boatman and 'uncle' to Michael.
Violet Hanney: 'Vi', 60, wife to Bill.
Joshua Hanney: 'Josh', 18, born Joshua Martin, sister to Caroline, 'adopted' as an orphan by Bill and Vi.

Steven Hanney: 'Stevie', 27, ex-boater, best friend of Michael and second son of Bill and Vi.
Eleanor Hanney: 'Ellie', 25, wife to Steven, born 'on the bank' in Knowle, Warwickshire.
Grace Hanney: 'Gracie', 7 months, daughter of Steven and Eleanor.

William Hanney: 'Billy', 32, boatman, oldest son of Bill and Vi.
Sylvia Hanney: 'Sylvie', 30, wife to Billy, born 'on the bank' in Alperton, West London.
Emily Hanney: 'Emmie', 8, daughter of Billy and Sylvie.
William Hanney: 'Little Bill', 6, son of Billy and Sylvie.
Violet Hanney: 3, second daughter of Billy and Sylvie.

Joseph Caplin: 'Joe', 35, oldest son of Henry and Suey (ex-boaters) and brother to Harriet and Samuel.
Grace Caplin: 'Gracie', 34, his wife and daughter of Bill and Vi Hanney.
Jack Caplin: 12, oldest son of Joe and Grace.
Rose Caplin: 'Rosie', 10, daughter of Joe and Grace.
Gabriel Caplin: 8, second son of Joe and Grace.
Henry Caplin: 6, third son of Joe and Grace.

Throughout my life, there has been someone who has been a constant presence. We haven't always seen eye to eye, but she has always been there when it mattered, becoming more like an extra Mum than a big sister:

For Jan

Part One

1957

August 14th 1957

Mr S. Hanney   Marloo Creek Station
42 Church Street   Mitchell,
Knowle   Qld, Australia
Warwickshire
England

Dear Stevie, Ellie and Grace,

  Well, here we are at last! It's been a long journey, and we're all very tired. The boat trip was a wonderful experience, worth it just for its own sake. We landed in Sydney a week ago, and stayed there overnight, then on the train to Brisbane, which took two days! It's difficult to understand just how huge a place Australia is. From Brisbane they flew us to a place called Toowoomba (some of the names here sound so strange to us!), and then on another smaller aeroplane to Mitchell, which is the nearest town to Marloo Creek. Sam, Ginny and Carrie have stayed behind in Toowoomba for a day or two, partly to rest but mainly because the little 'plane that

12

brought us here can only take a few people at once. Jerry O'Brien, who's the station manager here, picked us up from Mitchell the next morning and drove us here in a big Land Rover.

Like I said, you can't imagine how enormous this country really is. I said that Mitchell is the nearest town to Marloo Creek — it still took us over an hour to drive here, and that over dusty roads that hardly seemed to be there for a lot of the way! And Mitchell is not much of a town by our standards — there's just one street, with a couple of stores, a garage and a pub, where we stayed overnight before Jerry picked us up. But it's all there is — really! The next town of any size is a place called Roma, several hours away on a slightly better road from what Jerry says, back towards Toowoomba. The only thing about Mitchell that's big is the stock yards — what we would call the cattle market, where all the cattle are sold and taken away by train.

I don't know what I was expecting, but I felt quite disappointed at first when we got here. All there is at the side of the road is another dry track turning off and a kind of box on the top of a post where the mail is delivered and collected, with a rough wooden notice on it that says 'Marloo Creek'. You can't even see the buildings, such as they are, from the road! But it made us think when Jerry told us that we'd been driving along the edge of our land for a good part of the last hour. Our land! I still can't believe that all this is ours – and I don't really know just how big it is yet, either. Jerry is taking me for a tour of the boundary tomorrow, to see for myself – we're going to have to camp, as it will take us several days! And travel by horse, because a lot of the ground is too rough even for the Land Rover, which he calls 'the Ute'. Harrie and the children will stay here, of course, and try to get used to things.

The men have already demolished what was left of the house after the fire, and there's a big leveled area where they want to build us a new house. Nearby is the bunkhouse, where the men sleep, and they've cleaned up what used to be the old homestead, what they call a slab hut, made of what look like railway sleepers, for us to use until the new house is ready — they've gone to so much trouble for us! Even furnished it with stuff shipped over from Roma. There are paddocks behind the buildings, and a big stable for the horses (the men use them all the time on the station), and another big shed (about the size of your dad's house) for the machinery and the trucks. We've got our own water supply, which comes up from underground, pumped by a big windmill that stands over behind the stables. All the land around here looks pretty barren to our eyes — just a kind of bare scrubland, with dry-looking stunted trees scattered about. This is what the Australians call the Outback! But as Jerry says, there's so much of it that each station can be big enough to support a lot of cattle and sheep, so a place like Marloo Creek can make a lot of money as long as the weather plays ball! Apparently they get most of the rain in summer, but if that fails things can get a bit difficult — the pump (the bore as Jerry calls it) only really gives enough water for us, so if it gets too dry the cattle tend to suffer. Then again, he says it can go the other way too, with floods if there's too much rain at one time! Now is the middle of winter here, but it's still like a warm spring day to us even if it gets a bit chilly at night. They get a bit of frost once in a while; snow — what's that, they ask?

Jerry seems a really good man — he's a wiry little fellow, all brown and wrinkled from so long in the sun, with a strange accent that's half-Irish, half-Australian. He obviously knows his job — he'd been with my uncle here for fourteen years — and has a good relationship with the other hands, who are mostly white Australians (descended from European immigrants — or criminals! That's how Australia started)

16

with a couple of 'blackfellas', which is what they call the Aborigines. These fellows, according to Jerry, are good workers — he says many of the 'Abos' are unreliable, that they'll work fine for a while and then suddenly vanish into the bush. Apparently it's something to do with their old way of life, part of their tribal background, that they have this urge to go on 'walkabout', as they call it.

At the moment everything is so new and strange to us. The kids are loving it, so far, with so much space to play in and new things to see and do all the time, but I'm afraid they'll get bored all too soon with no-one else around. And I'm not sure about their education — if we decide to leave the boats for good, one of the reasons will be so that they can get some proper schooling, but there's no school within miles of us here! Jerry says they teach the station kids with lessons over the radio, but I'm not sure if I'm happy about that — I wonder how good it can be if there's no teacher to keep them working? I suppose that would come down to Harriet or me to see that they do their lessons. We'll give it a try while we're here, and see how it goes.

I suppose the big question in your minds is, are we going to stay here or come home? It's much too early to make up our minds yet, of course. Once we've got over the newness of it all, and we can see what life would be like here, we'll think about that. Jerry says that we'd have no trouble selling if we wanted to – but I get the feeling that he wants us to stay. He and I get on well, even after only one day together, and he seems to think the world of Harrie and the kids – he said to me this morning that it's so good to have children around, because it gives the place a future, and I think I can see what he means. I asked him how he felt about having a boss who knows nothing about cattle and sheep, and he just laughed and said that they'll soon get me trained! So we'll have to wait and see.

I guess that's about all for now. Harrie and the children send their love — write back and tell us the news from home. I don't know how long this will take to get to you, but the mail truck comes by here tomorrow (we get our post once a week!) so I'll send it and hope to hear from you soon.

All our best wishes,

Mikey.

August 26th 1957
Mr M. Baker   42 Church St
Marloo Creek Station   Knowle
Mitchell   Warks.
Queensland
Australia

Dear Mikey, Harriet, Alby, Susie and Freddie,

It was great to hear from you! Thanks for the letter – it took ten days to get to us here, so I guess this one will take about the same to get back to you. Three weeks altogether, just to exchange letters – it makes you realize just how far away you all are, doesn't it? We've missed you all, of course, but it's good to know that you're enjoying yourselves. How are things now? I expect you're more settled and are beginning to see what life would be like there. Have the others joined you? I suppose they will have by now! How do they like Australia? You sound quite impressed, but it must be so very different from here; I expect you're glad that you decided to give yourselves a month to look around before making up your minds whether to stay.

Everything here is pretty much the same as always. Our Gracie's been ill with the chicken-pox, but she's getting over it now. Dad and Stevie have been working all hours – with this rush to build new houses they've got so much work on they don't know

20

what to do! It's good, of course, because it means there's plenty of money coming in now that I'm not teaching any more, but I think Stevie's getting a bit fed up with it. He won't admit it, but he still misses the boats, I know – that was his whole life since he was born, after all, until we met. I sometimes feel a bit guilty for having taken him away from all of it – whenever we go to see Bill and Vi I can see the longing in his eyes as they talk about old times!

We went to Braunston last weekend, popped in to see Mr and Mrs Vickers and took a quick look at your boats. The Vickers' are fine and send their love; Olive said to thank you for their letter, and they'd write to you in the next day or two. The boats are fine, the men at Barlows yard are keeping an eye on them for you – we had some heavy rain a week ago, and they made a point of pumping them out afterwards, so you've no need to worry on that score!

The Transport Commission are trying to persuade Stevie's dad to retire – he's almost sixty-five, they reckon, so he's entitled to of course, but you know what he is! He say's that he doesn't want to sit on his bottom all day doing nothing, and he doesn't need their charity anyway – he's determined to go on working as long as he can. They've even told him he can stay in the house at the yard if he retires – they've got a new man lined up to be foreman there, and he's got a house in the town so they don't need it

– but he's digging his toes in. It looks as if this new man will have to wait for his promotion! Josh is still doing fine, and he's got a regular girlfriend now – did you meet her before you left? Pretty girl by the name of Laura, lives in Tilehouse Green, and he cycles over to see her after work most days.

We haven't heard from Joe and Gracie for a while, so you know as much about them as we do! I guess no news is good news, after the awful time they had losing little Henry; it sounds as though Gabriel is back to normal now, thank goodness! Billy and Sylvie seem to be doing well – we haven't seen them either, but they did stop in to see Bill and Vi not long ago. They're still working for Waterways, carrying loads of steel from Brentford to Birmingham and coal back from the mines around Coventry to the papermills at Croxley. The kiddies are growing up, and you can see the pride in Vi's face when she talks about them!

Well, I can't think of anything else to say for now. I hope everything is still going well for you – write again and tell us more about Australia, and the farm you've inherited! Everyone here sends their love – Bill and Vi, my Mum and Dad and our Jim (he goes back to university next week), Billy and Sylvie and the children (via Bill), and Stevie of course. We're all eager to hear what you decide – I know all of us will miss you if you decide to stay, but at the same time we want you to do whatever is best for you and the children, for the future, and we will always be behind you, whatever happens.

With our love,

Ellie Hanney.

September 12th 1957

Marloo Creek Stn
Mitchell Qld.

Mr & Mrs S.Hanney
42 Church Street
Knowle
Warwickshire
England

Dear Stevie, Ellie and Gracie,

      Thanks for the letter. After a month in Australia, it was good to hear about the folks back home. Harrie and I were talking about you all last night, with Sam and Ginny, and it's strange but our whole lives in England seem so long ago — but at the same time it's as if it was only yesterday we were loading at Pooley Hall or Griff, or shoveling coal into the conveyor at Croxley! It feels odd to know that that is all still going on while we're sitting here in the sun, so far away.

      Things here are looking good for us — as far as we can see at the moment, anyway. I'm learning a lot about the sheep and cattle business from going around with Jerry, and the other hands are all being really great — they don't seem to mind that I'm a complete idiot when it comes to the job here! They're all being very patient with me, helping me to get the feel of what goes on. Sam's joining in, of course — if we do all stay, he'll end up working here the same as me. Harrie and Ginny are settling in to the outback way of life — it does come as a shock when you realize that you can't just go to the nearest shops for the odd things you've run out of. Each shopping expedition has to be organized like a military campaign, planned carefully with lists of everything we need.

And we've enrolled the kids in that radio school set-up — it seems to be working fine, and they really love it, although that might be because it's still so new to them. They've got a tutor who looks after them, and that's great — much better than sitting in a class with thirty or so other kids! And they like the idea that they can do a lot of their work at times when they want to — they can be outside and play in the sunshine during the day, and then sit and study or write essays in the evening when it gets colder. Their written work has to be posted off to the tutor, and then it comes back in the post, marked and with helpful notes added.

I expect you're wondering about Carrie, too? Well, we have a surprise for you! On their way to join us here, she and Sam and Ginny stayed in the pub in Mitchell too — and she's taken a shine to son of the owners! After all the time she's been getting over losing her Charlie Nixon, suddenly she's full of beans again, bouncing around like a little kid! She spends half her time in the town, staying at the pub where she works part-time as what they call a 'glassy' — her job is to collect the empty glasses and wash them ready to be used again. We've met her Davey, of course — he seems like a really nice lad, and Harrie thinks he's really stuck on her too. If this romance goes on, we can see her deciding to stay here whatever we do!

As to that — we still can't make up our minds. I know it sounds like we're avoiding the question, but we're going to stay another few weeks before we decide. That'll let us see how serious Carrie is with this lad, and give us all time to get a better idea of what life will be like here long-term. It will be so difficult! I'm beginning to think that Australia might be a better place for the future, especially for the kids when they grow up — there seem to be so many opportunities for them here — but then it will be so hard to leave you all behind, to accept that it might be many years before we see you again.

We're grateful for what you said in your letter, about backing us whatever we decide to do, it does help us feel a bit less as though we're deserting you all if we do stay. And Harrie had a letter from her parents (they got their next door neighbour to write for them) in this weeks post as well as yours, and they say exactly the same thing — I know she's finding it difficult to think of leaving them, with her dad's back getting so bad, but he told her in the letter that she's got to do what's best for us and our kiddies, that they'll be fine on their own. She had a little cry over that, but I think it helped her too.

If we do stay, of course we'll have to sell the boats. I expect Ben would do that for us, but I don't know what they're worth now — there were so many boats lying around everywhere that I don't suppose they'll fetch much at all. Not that we need the money! After so many years of having to manage on what I earned on the boats, its seems so strange not to have to worry about that any more — the station here earns more than we could spend however hard we tried! I had to laugh — in your letter, you called it a farm, and I suppose in English terms that's what it would be, but to call something the size of a small county a farm just seems so funny to us! In Australia, they're known as stations, or sometimes just properties — it's funny how quickly you get into the local way of thinking and talking about things.

Harrie and I are having a weekend off this week, taking the children for a couple of days back to Toowoomba. Jerry's going to drive us to Mitchell, and we'll arrange for the aeroplane to pick us up there; we'll come back on Monday, maybe stay overnight in Mitchell with Carrie at the pub. Sam and Ginny are going to stay here — it'll give Sam a taste of being in charge! Although of course it's Jerry who pretty well runs things around here — we're just the apprentices, even if we do own the place.

I still can't get that idea into my head, you know? We, Harrie and I, and Sam and Ginny, we actually own this land, these cattle and sheep — it seems like a fantastic dream! That's the other question — would we want to give this all up now we've found it? It would get a huge price, enough to live on for years and years, but it feels wrong somehow to turn our backs on it now that fortune has given it to us, and to me at least like letting down my uncle and aunt who spent their lives building it all up from nothing. We're back to that question again, aren't we? We will decide, quite soon, and you'll be the first to know, I promise!

Please give our love to everyone at home — we have written to them all, and I expect we'll hear from them soon. Susie says to give Gracie a big kiss for her.

With all our love,

Mikey.

September 25th 1957   42 Church St
                                      Knowle

Mr & Mrs M. Baker
Marloo Creek Station
Mitchell, Qld.

Dear Mikey, Harrie, Alby, Susie and
Freddie,

    Thanks for the letter. It's good to
hear that things are going well for you all.
Did you enjoy your weekend off? What do
Sam and Ginny think of life in Australia?
And is Carrie still sweet on that fellow from
the pub?

    I think Ellie told you in her last
letter that her dad and I are working all
hours at the moment. There's such a big
need for new houses, and that means all
the timber work that goes with them, like
making roof frames and floor joists not to
mention things like doors and windows.
It's good, of course - we're earning lots of
money - but to be honest it's pretty boring.
I like working for Mr Carter, we get on very
well and he's been so good to Ellie and me,
but I am missing life on the boats more
and more as time goes by. I'm not sure

31

what to do, Mikey - I've got a good well-paid job, but I'm really not very happy, and I know that Ellie knows that and it's making her unhappy too. But then we owe James so much that I feel as if to leave would be letting him down - you know what I mean? Ellie's Mum Amanda is so sweet too, and I'd hate to upset her. They both dote on our Gracie, as you can imagine! Anyhow, that's our problem, and you've got enough to think about without listening to my worries.

We saw Billy and Sylvie the other day - I was still at work, but Ellie got a phone call from Mum to say that they'd stopped there for the night with a load of steel for Sampson Road, so she got a message to us at work and we went over to see them. It was really great, tucking in to one of Mum's enormous stews and chatting about the old days! Dad, Billy and me got through quite a few bottles of beer, so Ellie had to drive home. Their kids are all fine, growing up so quickly - Emmie's eight now, of course, and a pretty little girl. Takes after her mother, luckily for her! Little Bill's super, but he's a bit of a tearaway - he reminds me of your Alby; and they chose the right name for little Violet - she's just like a tiny version of my Mum! They all made a big fuss over our Gracie, especially little Vi. Sylvie's taken a leaf out of your book, Mikey - she's teaching the kids to read and write, and insists that they all go to school whenever the boats are tied up for a day anywhere.

Gracie's fine now - we were quite worried about her when she had the chicken-pox, I think Ellie told you, but she got over it okay in the end. She's eight months old now - the time seems to be flying by! Sleeps right through the night now, thank goodness, it was getting very difficult trying to work all day and then getting woken up at all times of the night.

Ben says your boats are still okay. He pops down to take a look at them every day or two, and the men at Barlows are keeping an eye on them too - he said Max, the foreman painter, was asking how you were the other day when he rang us. You knew that James had put the telephone in for us, didn't you? He said he'd pay the bills as well, but I couldn't let him do that, could I? He did arrange it all, though, and it's been very useful, not just for work but it means we can keep in touch with Mum and Dad, because he's got the company telephone in their house.

We had a letter from Gracie the other day. Joe's left the Post Office, he's driving a lorry for Pickford's now, moving furniture for people and things like that. She says they're all okay now, but that they do miss little Henry so much - I can guess how they feel, I know how I'd be if anything happened to our Grace! Thank goodness little Gabriel got over the TB, I can't imagine what it would be like to lose two kiddies! He's as bouncy as ever now - he'll be nine soon, can you imagine? He and Jack and Rosie all go to school in Hemel Hempstead - Jack went up to his new school this month. It doesn't seem possible that he can be twelve now, does it? Ellie's written back and suggested that they come and see us on the train soon, maybe when the kids have their half-term holiday - it'll be good to see them, I haven't seen my big sister since Easter! Have you heard from them? She said they'd had a letter from you.

Well, I guess I haven't got anything else to tell you. I hope you're all well, and still enjoying yourselves. I expect you'll be making your minds up about what to do very soon now? Like Ellie told you before, you must do whatever you think is right for you all. We'll miss you if you stay there, but we can always write, and maybe we'll come and visit you one day? Or I expect you'll come back here sometime, for a holiday, right? So it's not for ever, whatever you do, we will see you again sometime.

Ellie and Gracie send their love;
All the best,
Steve.

Mikey – In your letter you said about selling the boats if you do stay in Australia. If you do stay, would you consider selling them to us? I know how unhappy Stevie is at the moment, how much he'd like to go back on the canals. I don't know if we can make a go of it the way you and Harrie did, or even if I can be a boater! But if the chance is there, I think we've got to try, otherwise Stevie will always be wondering 'what if' – you know what I mean! I'm not sure if I'll be able to do the work and look after Gracie at the same time, but I've got to make the effort, for his sake. And he doesn't know it, but my Dad is aware that he's not happy the way things are, so he won't be too upset about it. Disappointed, maybe, but he'll understand, I know. By the way, Stevie doesn't know I'm slipping this note to you in with his letter, so don't say anything, all right? I'll cross that bridge when we get to it!

Love, Ellie.

October 11th 1957   Marloo Creek
Mr & Mrs S. Hanney   Qld.
42 Church Street
Knowle

Dear Steve and Ellie,

Well, this is it! We've been here two months now, all but, and it's time to make up our minds. First, though, thank you for your letter, Stevie — it was good to get the news of everyone back home, especially Billy and Sylvie. It sounds as though they're still doing all right, getting plenty of orders, and it's good to know the kids are all doing well — I know what you mean about Little Bill, when you say he's like our Alby, they've got the same cheeky sense of humour, but he reminds me more of his dad when he was younger! Yes, we did get a letter from Gracie and Joe — I didn't know that she'd learnt to read and write as well — had to, I expect, so that she could keep up with the kids! We hadn't seen them for a while before we left, and didn't have the time in the rush to set

37

off, but I always did like young Jack — I hope Alby and Freddie turn out such good kids as he is as they get older. Like you say, it seems incredible that he's up in big school now. I never made it that far! Joe says that his Dad is getting quite poorly now, with his back, they've given him a wheelchair but he only uses it when he has to, and then under protest!   That upset Harrie a bit as you'll understand, but Joe also said that Henry is still adamant that we should stay here if we think it's best for us and the kids.

I take it that your Mum and Dad are all right? Has he decided to retire, or is he going to stick to his guns and carry on?   I can't imagine him sitting at home all day! Or your Mum coping if he's under her feet all the time — I remember when I was with you after your Dad and Billy saved me from the canal, how she was the one who ran the 'home' side of your life on the boats, and I can just see her getting all exasperated with him when he gets in her way! She was the one who suggested passing me on to my Dad,

Alby — did you know that? I owe her so much!

But I suppose I'd better stop beating about the bush and get to the real point of this letter. We had a big family talk last night, me and Harrie, Sam and Ginny, and we insisted that Carrie was there as well although it's difficult to get her away from Mitchell these days. We talked for ages, going round and round in circles for a lot of the time, but in the end, although it does make us all sad in a lot of ways, we are going to stay. Sam and I have both learnt a lot about running a wool and cattle station, and Jerry is happy with us and keen for us to stay here — and I think we're both eager to see how well we can do. We've got plans, with Jerry's advice, to expand the business, and we think things can only get better for all of us. Harrie and Ginny are both happy to stay and run the home between them — Jerry has suggested that we rebuild the main house for Harrie and me and the kids, and build another one for Sam and Ginny, so we'll all have our privacy and some independence. The kids still love it here — they're enjoying the climate, after the cold and damp of England, but as Jerry says they might find it harder in the summer, when it can get really hot. And the radio school seems to suit them, probably better than if they'd gone to a normal school after the freedom of living on the boats. So everything is fair dinkum, as they say here!

What about Carrie, you'll be wondering — well, we've got more news for you there, too. Davey Watson has asked her to marry him! It all seems a bit too quick, for my liking, especially when these things always took so long on the boats — but then, as Harrie says, we didn't get to see each very often, so she's probably spent more time with this lad than we did together before we got married. They're both really set on the idea, and Harrie seems happy for them to go ahead, and I'm sure she's a better judge of this sort of thing than I am. We've met him a number of times now, and he does seem a really nice boy; he's twenty-one, a year older than her, and works in a big timber-yard out in the bush the other side of Mitchell. Mrs Watson, his Mum, runs the pub, and she's very pleased with Carrie and seems more than happy to have her as a daughter-in-law — I gather Davey's been unlucky with girlfriends in the past, got in with a girl who was only out to rook him for all she could get. Anyway, we've decided to give them our blessing if they're certain about it, but they've agreed to wait for a bit before actually arranging everything. We'll let you know what happens!

I'll be writing to everyone else back home over the next day or two, but as I promised, you're the first to know! Next letter will be to Ben Vickers — he's written a couple of times, and said that both Willow Wren and Waterways have been asking if our boats are available for sub-contract loads. Which brings me to the next thing: I know you're not happy carpentering, Stevie — how would you like to be back on the cut?

41

I'm sure that Mr Carter would understand if you wanted to go back. Like I said before, I don't suppose the boats would fetch a lot of money if we sold them anyway – you can have them, if you want them, as long as you promise to look after them! You'd be best advised to find yourself a mate, I think – after all, Ellie's not a boater, and it would be difficult for you with just the two of you. And you've got Gracie to look after – I'm sure there must be a few likely lads about if you ask around. What do you think? Take your time to think about it for a bit, if you want, there's no hurry – talk to Mr Carter and his wife, see what they say, and to Ben as well, he'll give you good advice the same as he always did to me. And your Dad, of course – no need to ask your brother – we all know what he'll say! It's up to you and Ellie, of course – decision time for both of us, Stevie! Now that ours is made, if you want to take advantage of things we'd be only too happy for you to do that. You've always been my best mate, and it would be good to know that you're taking over the *Albert* and the *Rita*, keeping them working the way they should be. Think about it, and let us know when you're ready.

In the meantime, we've got so much to do! Sam, Jerry and I have got to set about designing the new houses, getting all the stuff together and building them — homes here are mostly built of wood, and that's where young Davey can come in useful! And we've still got the station to run. All four of us are learning to drive — we can't be dependent on Jerry all the time, and Sam and I will need to be able to get around the place on our own anyway. Once they're happy, the girls will be able to run into Mitchell for the shops every week, which will free everyone up — we depend on one of the men doing it at the moment, when they could be more use back here.

If you see your Mum and Dad, or any of the others, tell them we're writing to them too — our post goes today, and if I hurry I can just about get this letter to the box in time.   Give everyone our love, say that we're thinking of them.

              All the best,

                        Mikey.

October 23rd 1957

Mikey

Now I've sat down with pen and paper, I don't know what to say. Let me start with the easy bit! Thanks for your letter - we sat down and talked about it last night, Ellie and me, and James and Amanda, and we all think you've done the right thing. Australia is a new country, and there must be so many opportunities for you all - it sounds as though Marloo Creek is a business on the up and up from what you say, and we all wish you nothing but success in the years to come. We're going to miss you, of course, but we can cope with that as long as we know you're happy and doing well.

But the boats - Mikey, it's a wonderful offer, but I need to think about things a bit before we decide what to do. I know you'll understand. And anyway, I can't just take them, that wouldn't be at all fair - you and Harriet have put so much into them, and you paid a good price for them in the first place, so I'll have to pay you for them. It's so generous of you to try and give them to me, but I can't do that, it wouldn't seem right. I spoke to Dad on the phone last night, and he says the same - I hope you're not upset? You're a boater, and I'm sure you know how I feel.

I'd love to go back on the cut, you're quite right about that! But I've got Ellie and Gracie to think about. Gracie must go to school when she's older, we've got to give her the best education we can - that's the only way kids will get on in the world the way things are now. And hopefully we'll have more children as time goes by, too. Give us a few days to talk about it, and I'll write again soon. James says he won't mind if I leave the firm and go back to the boats, but I can see that he's a bit upset about it, so I've got to talk to him a lot more about things. I'll let you know just as soon as I can.

In the mean time, Mikey, thank you so much for your generous offer. Ellie sends her love and her thanks too, and Mum and Dad said to say hello. We all hope you'll be very happy with your new life.

Cheerio,
Steve.

Mikey – just a quick note from me too, to say thank you! If I could I'd give you a big hug and a kiss or six – tell Harriet she'll have to do that for me. I wish you could have seen Stevie's face when he read your letter, the bit about the boats! Now the chance is there, I know he's almost desperate to go back on the canal – I'm sure my Dad will agree, he's already as good as said so, and I wouldn't be surprised if he doesn't help Stevie with the money, as well. After all, he is my Dad!

Please give our love to Harriet and the children, and Sam and Ginny and Carrie – it's wonderful to know that she's found someone at last, after such a dreadful time over Charlie, wish her all the happiness in the world, from all of us. And Mikey – thank you, thank you, thank you!

All my love,
Ellie.

November 6th 1957   *42 Church St*
                                      Knowle

Dear Mikey, Harriet and the kids,

I don't know if you might have written back after my last letter, but I thought I should write anyway, to let you know as soon as possible what we're going to do. I took your advice, and went to see Ben Vickers first - he always seems to have the most balanced view of things on the cut. He's not keen to go on arranging orders for us like he did for you, but then as Olive says he's over seventy now, and it's about time he took things easy. I can't blame him! And as he says, everything you were doing in the last few years was subbing for someone else - he rang Waterways for us, and they've said that they can use the boats if they're available, for us to just report in at Bulls Bridge or Suttons and they'll give us orders in rotation with any other boats that are waiting, so that looks okay. And he told me he'd heard from you, that you'd said if I wouldn't take the boats for nothing to sell them to me for a good cheap price - you knew I wouldn't be happy to just take

48

them, didn't you? We had a kind of reverse auction, me trying to make him take more money and him talking me down all the time! But we've agreed a price that we're both happy with now.

Dad's right behind us as well - he's not certain how long the trade will go on, he says he sees less and less boats about as time goes by, but as he says we've both got an education - Ellie more than me, of course! - so we can go back on the bank if it gets difficult to make a living. Both he and Ben are asking around to see if we can get a suitable young lad as mate; Ellie and Gracie will come with me to begin with, but we're thinking that she might go back home with her parents when Gracie needs to go to school. Or maybe Gracie could live with Grannie and Grandad, and come with us in the holidays. Billy thinks it's great for us to go back on the cut, of course - we saw them at Dad's last night. They tied up there, and Mum had been to the shops and got some fireworks - it was Guy Fawke's Night, and the kids all enjoyed the show Dad put on in the garden.

Sorry, Mikey - you will have gathered by now that we're taking up your offer of going back on the boats! James seems happy about it, although he says he'll miss me in the business, and Amanda insists that we must do what will make us happy. Young Jimmie's quite thrilled - he's got ideas of coming with us when he's not at college! Not that young really - he was twenty this year, finishes at University next summer. James is going to lend us the money for the boats, by the way. We were going to sell the house, but he suggests we keep it and rent it out - makes sense, we might need it again one day ourselves, and it'll give us a bit of money coming in in the meantime.

So, that's it. Ben's having Barlows give the boats a docking before we actual take them over, so it'll be a few weeks before we actually start work. End of this month, probably. I can't wait, and even Ellie seems quite excited, although I think she's a bit scared of the idea of looking after Gracie in such a small space as a boat cabin! She'll cope, she's that kind of girl - and after all, Mum brought three of us up on the boats - four, if you count poor Jackie.

Which reminds me - we had a letter from Grace the other day. Sounds like their Jack is doing well in his new school, thoroughly enjoying himself, and the other kids are doing fine. She's got a job as a dinner-lady in their school, the younger ones that is, so with Joe driving his lorries they're quite well off these days. And Josh is okay, working hard at his apprenticeship, but he's fallen out with Laura, got a new girlfriend we haven't met yet.

Well, I guess that's about all I've got to tell you. We're both so grateful to you, Mikey, for the offer of the boats - we'll make the best go of it we can! And we all hope you and Harriet, and Sam and Ginny and the children will be very happy in your new lives, too.

All the best,

Steve.

November 19th 1957   Marloo Creek
                                   Qld

42 Church St
Knowle

Dear Stevie,

      Thanks for your letter — it's great news! We're all so pleased that you're going back on the cut, and everyone here wishes you well. I'm sure you'll make a go of it, you've always been about the best boater I know — you taught me a lot, on that first trip to Birnigum, remember? They were great times, weren't they? Let us know how you get on, how Ellie likes life on the boats — it'll be a huge change for her, as I know only too well! And I was just a kid, it was easier for me to cope with — and of course I wanted to get away from my old home, so I was eager for the change. Give her all our love, won't you? I'm sure your Mum'll help her all she can, with advice and tips and the like.

Things are coming on here too. We've roughed out designs for the new houses, and Jerry's organizing getting the materials together. We'll start building as soon as possible, because it's pretty cramped here at the moment — not like the boats, maybe, but Harrie and I and the kids are crammed into the old slab hut, and Sam and Ginny are having to manage in a room in the bunkhouse. We've been and bought another ute, a brand-new Chevrolet, now that Sam and I can both drive, we need another car really. It's a funny looking thing, the front part is just like a big motor-car, but it stops just behind the front doors and there's an open truck bed built on the back. It's great to drive — got a big 6-cylinder engine, so it's much faster than the old Land Rovers, and Jerry reckons it'll be tough enough to cope with the dirt-tracks around here.

We've had some rain lately, which is good as things were getting a bit dry. Jerry was looking a bit worried, although he didn't say anything, but he's back to grinning from ear to ear again now that the creek's running well. We've got a creek running right across the property — well, I guess the name of the place might have given you a clue! That's the water supply for the stock, while I think I told you we've got a bore here for the homestead. The creek was down to a trickle for a week or two, but there's a lot more water there now.

Just over a month to Christmas — it seems so strange to be thinking of Christmas in the middle of summer! It's made us all think of home, and we're getting a bit nostalgic I suppose. Harrie and I are going to miss the boats, I know — we already do. We both loved the life, and I think she envies you two as much as I do. What we both agree we won't miss is the cold and the rain, the snow and ice in the winter — it's amazing how quickly we've got used to being warm all the time, even when it does rain!

We've so much to do here, and that idea is so exciting! And we both think that the children will have a much better future here. They've adapted to things here so well – Alby and Susie are still enjoying their radio school, and doing well; Freddie will join in next year, when he's four. They're all as brown as berries, and spend as much time as they can out of doors – it's a job to get Alby to put his shirt on, but as Jerry says the sun here is so strong that it can do you a lot of harm if you overdo it. We've all taken to wearing hats most of the time – Sam and I could almost pass as Aussies with our bush hats on! We're getting quite good on the horses, too – Harrie was very nervous at first, but she's fine now, actually goes out with Ginny for a ride some afternoons. And the kids all love the horses – even Freddie sits on the smallest of the ponies and trots around the yard, with Susie leading him.

Well, that's all our news. I suppose you'll be working by the time you get this letter – I'll send it to your Mum's, that way I know she'll see that you get it. Do write and let us know how things go – we'll be thinking of you, slogging along through the snow! We do really hope it all goes well for you, Stevie — and do give Ellie our love, and little Gracie. And say hello to your Mum and Dad, and tell Josh that Carrie sends her love. She and Davey are planning to get married next year, in September, by the way.

We do miss you all, but then maybe we'll be able to come back home for a holiday one day. Look after yourselves, and say hello to everyone on the cut for us.

Best wishes,

Mikey.

December 14th 1957

Hello Mikey, Harrie, Sam, Ginny, and the children

     Merry Christmas! Just taking the time while we're waiting at Bull's Bridge for orders to drop you a quick line – I hope you'll get this in time. It will seem strange, having Christmas without you all around, but we hope you'll have a good time out there in the sun. As you said in your letter, it must be very odd to be sitting down to Christmas dinner in the warmth and sunshine. Enjoy yourselves, and give a thought to us stuck here in the cold!

     The weather's been all right, so far this winter. Not too cold, but pretty wet over the last few weeks. And the wind! Steve put off setting out from Braunston for a day when the boats were ready because it was so windy, and he says that they're difficult to handle in the wind when they're empty. I didn't understand then, but we got caught in the wind again, running empty from Birmingham to Sutton's, and I soon found out! We had to do that first trip on our own, and I had a terrible time trying to keep the butty straight behind the motor, especially on that stretch above Atherstone locks where it's so exposed. We got there, though! We'd had a load of steel from Brentford to Sampson Road, then went to load coal from Newdigate for Dickinson's paper mill at Croxley.

We've got our mate now, which will make things much easier. You remember Jack and Maggie Warden, and their family? Steve says their oldest, Kim, used to work with Billy and Sylvie – he's left the cut now, working in a car factory in Birmingham somewhere. Jack and Maggie have left too – the middle boy, Terry, was killed in Denham Deep Lock, I don't know if you'd heard? He was single-handing a spare motor boat down to Bull's Bridge, following his Mum and Dad, and they lost track of him behind them. Jack went back to see if he was all right, and found him in the empty lock, floating beside the boat. They think he'd jumped down onto the roof and slipped – it was wet and raining – gone in and drowned. Anyway, Jack and Maggie didn't want to go on any more, so they've got a little cottage in Harefield. Their youngest boy, Nicky, didn't like it on the bank, so he's coming with us – we picked him up on the way down after unloading at Croxley. He's nice kid, polite and keen, just turned fourteen. He's living in the motor cabin, and Steve and I have the butty.

I'm beginning to see why you boaters all loved this life! I suppose it's different if you're born to it, been doing it all your life, but it's so new and exciting for me. Oh, it's hard work, and dirty sometimes – I got really filthy helping Steve to shovel coal at Croxley! But it's great to be out in the open air so much, I feel more alive than I have for years, especially after stuffy schoolrooms. And Gracie seems happy, too, and I'm sure it's healthier for her, even if it's difficult to look after her the way I'm used to in such a small space. But I'm getting used to it! We're both happier than we've been for ages – and so grateful to you for giving us this opportunity, Mikey.

It was a Sunday when we came through Boxmoor, on our way down here for the first time with the empty boats, and we stopped there for a while to meet up with Joe and Grace and their children. It'd been a while since we'd seen them, and they wanted to see us and wish us well. We had a drink in the Fishery Inn, and a good old chat! The kids are all growing up – Jack's getting to be a fine young lad, and Rosie's a real sweetie. Gabriel's lovely, but he's a bit too lively for me, always rushing around, he never seems to stop! Nearly nine! I'm sure I could see envy in Joe's eyes, but he says he doesn't regret leaving the boats – he's got a good job, well paid, and now Grace's working too they're doing well. They send their love, of course.

My Mum and Dad and Jimmy, and Steve's folks, all send their love too. We'll all be thinking of you over the holiday – take care and enjoy yourselves.
All my love
Ellie.

59

Interlude

1962

July 22nd 1962

Top Lock Cottage
Knowle
Warks.

Mr & Mrs Baker
Marloo Creek Station
Mitchell
Queensland
Australia

Dear Mikey, Harriet and the kids,

Thanks for your last letter. Time just seems to fly by, doesn't it? I can't believe that Alby's twelve already, I suppose I still think of him as the little boy he was when you left England. And Susie, coming up to eleven! She looks a really pretty little girl in the pictures, you must be so proud of them all! I'll get a card and present in the post for Freddie in good time for his birthday, I promise!

Gracie's a bit nervous about starting school this year, but I'm sure she'll be all right once she gets there and starts to make new friends. Now that The Bump is getting bigger, I've left Stevie and Nicky to work the boats – Gracie and I are going to stay with Bill and Vi, in their house, where we can be by the canal and see them when they come past. We've still got the little car, so I can run her into school every day – you probably remember that we left it here so that Bill could use it, when we went on the boats. Almost five years ago – how can it be so long? I'm

62

going to miss that life – I know we had our hard times, but I've enjoyed it so much. But now the children come first, and Stevie is insistent that Gracie must have a good education – and with The Bump getting close to arriving, he wants us to be safely on the bank.

I don't know how long they will go on boating, to be honest, Mikey. We've been just about getting enough orders to keep us going, but there seem to be more and more of the loads being sent by lorry these days. There's still the demand for coal from around the Coventry area, down to Dickinson's paper mills and the Ovaltine factory, and we've usually had a back-load from Brentford, steel or other metals to Sampson Road or around Birmingham, or sometimes timber to Tyseley. And we did a few trips with grain down to Whitworth's, on the River Nene – hard work, all those narrow locks on the Northampton arm! Stevie's keen to keep working, and at the moment things seem to be going steadily enough, but I can't help wondering what the future holds. I guess the biggest shock for you will be if I tell you that Barlows have given up! They were down to six pairs working, and a little while ago they sold out to a fellow called Michael Streat. He runs a little business at Braunston, hiring out cabin cruisers to people for holidays, seems to be doing quite well at it, and now he's bought what was left of the Barlows fleet. They're still going, but only using lorries now – Blue Line, as this other fellow calls himself, is going to carry on whatever contracts Barlows had on the canal.

Bill is going to retire next month – the company have finally told him he's got to! He's nearly seventy, so it's about time – but you know what he's like. Like a lot of old boaters, he's not actually sure exactly how old he really is, or even when his birthday is, and that's how he's managed to fight them off for so long, but even the people at Waterways can work out that he must be that age by now! He's as fit and strong as ever, bless him, and I'm sure he'll find something to keep him busy – I hope so, for Vi's sake, I can't imagine her putting up with him under her feet all the time! She's fine, as well, but I think she's feeling her age more that he is, to be truthful. She sometimes complains of feeling tired all the time, but still she won't take things any easier than ever.

Josh is doing well – nearly at the end of his apprenticeship, and back with his Laura – did you know? Billy and Sylvie are doing fine - we saw them a little while ago, just after Violet's birthday – eight now! Linda's toddling around, getting into everything like any two-year-old and driving her Dad to distraction; Emily and Little Bill are fine too, working hard at their lessons – Sylvie's doing a marvelous job of teaching them, and I've been helping where I can by suggesting the kind of things I used when I was teaching, books and so on. And watching Bill on the boats is a treat – I swear he's a better boater than his Dad, but I wouldn't dare tell Billy that!

Joe and Grace send their love – Jack's at college now, studying English and Maths, doing very well, Joe says. Rosie's just finished her GCE's, thinks she's done all right – and Gabriel is still hankering after that pet kangaroo! He's such a nice boy now, calmed down a lot as he's got older, as polite and thoughtful a kid as you could wish for – going to drama classes as well, now. They came to see us last week, on the Sunday, when they heard that I'd left the boats, and by pure good luck picked a weekend when Stevie was here too, on his way to Sampson Road.

Well, I guess that's about all the family news. Stevie's scribbled a letter for you, before they left today and I'll put it in with mine – he'll tell you more about what they're up to with the boats. Bill and Vi send their love, as do my Mum and Dad – Jimmy's off working in Sheffield now, but I'm sure he'd want to say hello too.

Take care of yourselves,
All my love,
Ellie

Top Lock Cottage
Knowle
July 22nd

Dear Mikey,

How are you, Mate? We're on our way up to Sampson Road again, copper ingots this time, then it'll be back to Sutton's and more coal for Croxley or Home Park or somewhere. Just stopped by to see Mum and Dad, and Ellie - she's living with them now, so that G can go to school in September. She says she's going to write to you, so I expect she'll tell you all about that. And what she calls 'the bump' is getting bigger - due early September as well, so it looks like Dad might be the one taking littl'un to school when she starts! I know she could do what Sylvie is, and teach Gracie on the boats, but I don't really want that - I think she'll need a good schooling for her future, and her little brother or sister, too. I'm missing them both, of course, but Nicky's good company and we can work the boats quite well on our own. As long as we don't get back on the wheat run! We did a few trips with wheat from Brentford to Whitworth's, on the Wellingborough River - the river's okay, but there's the 17 narrow locks of that dratted arm! They sometimes have a horse there to pull the butty down, but you can't rely on it.

We're getting a steady run of orders, not having to hang about too long most of the time, but things are not getting any better. Talking to people and keeping your eyes open you can see that more and more stuff is going on the lorries now - you know that Barlow's have given up? They're just running lorries themselves now, sold the last six pairs to Mr Streat. He's been hiring out cabin cruisers to people for holidays for a year or two now, calls it Blue Line Cruisers, and now he's taken on the last two contracts that Barlow's had - coal to the Jam 'ole at Southall and sand from Leighton Buzzard - most of that goes to Birnigum but a bit goes down to London too. Ernie Kendall was telling me all about it when we met them in the Nelson a few weeks ago - he's on with his mum and Arthur, with the Roger and the Raymond. Sounds like steady work.

Biggest problem we have all the time is dealing with the depots - the bloody dockers union seems to spend half it's time trying to come up with ways to make life difficult for the boaters! You remember what they were like - they're just as awkward about things now. We're used to it at Brentford, but the men around the Birnigum depots are as bad now. Only the other week we unloaded at Sampson Road, then went to Tyseley for a load of cocoa waste, but the men there sent us back to Sampson Road, who sent us back to Tyseley - talk about the left hand not knowing what the right hand's doing! We eventually got our load of cocoa - they ship it off abroad somewhere, and it gets turned into face-cream or something, or so the lighterman told us when they unloaded it. And the state of the cut's no better than it was when you were here - there's hardly any dredging being done, and they're letting trees grow all along the offside, hanging out into the channel and dropping their leaves into the water every year so the cut gets shallower than ever.

Sorry, I'm sounding like - what was it you called that guy in your letter, the English fella who was always complaining - a whinging Pom! On a happier note, we had an interesting little job a while back.

The church in Knowle approached Dad to see if he could arrange a boat trip for them, so of course he got hold of us! We picked them up at the bridge, just above the locks, and took them down as far as that winding hole a bit past Hatton Tunnel. They had their own picnic with them, and the weather was great, so everyone had a good time - 113 people at 2/6d each, £14 2/6d for a day's work! We don't make that in two weeks as a rule! Dad said we should give up carrying coal and carry people instead.

They're saying that things are going to change on the cut next year. The old Transport Commission's being done away with, and there's going to be a new lot running the canals. We don't know much yet, but we're all hoping that it'll improve things - they can't get much worse! We'll have to wait and see, I suppose - it reminds me of when they nationalized it all, do you remember? Everybody was saying that it'd sort things out, get the dredging done and so on, but it never happened, did it? Maybe this lot'll be the same - but you have to hope, don't you? Sorry, I'm moaning again! Not like me usually - but to be honest, Mikey, I'm a bit worried about Mum. She's looking very tired lately, and admits that she doesn't have the energy she used to, puts it down to just getting old. She might be right, but I can't help feeling that there's more to it. But you know what she is - she won't go to the doctor.

Anyway, Mate, that's about all I've got to say for now. Glad to hear you're all doing so well out there. Love to Harrie and Ginny and the kids, say hello to Sam - how's Carrie these days?

All the best,

Steve.

Part Two

1963

New Year's Day, 1963
The White Lion, Marsworth

Dear Mikey and all,

Well, another New Year! I only hope this one's going to get better as it goes on! Nicky and me had got to Marsworth bottom with a load of coal for Nash Mills on Christmas Eve, so we left the boats there and both got the train home. It was bloody cold all over Christmas, and when we got back on Boxing Day everywhere was frozen solid. We've had a hard frost every night since, and heavy snow too, so the boats are still stuck where we left them. I sent Nicky home again after a couple of days, because it seemed pointless both of us sitting here going nowhere - I can get hold of him, one of their neighbours has a telephone and I can call from the pub, if it looks like thawing. I hope it won't be too long - we've got no money coming in while we're stuck here, that's the one thing about running your own boats, isn't it? Not like '47, when we had the laying money from Fellows's. But it could be much worse - we have got the rent money from the house. You know we kept it when we went back on the boats? The first tenants we had in there were a nightmare! Wrecked the place, and then the agents had a fight getting them out. Cost us all the money they'd paid in rent to put it right afterwards, even with James doing a lot of the work. He's been so great to us, all along, but at least we've been able to pay him back the money he lent us to buy the boats now! Anyway, the people in there now are very good - Maurice is a middle-aged guy who works for James, and his wife is a part-time nurse. They've got two grown-up kids, both married and gone, and they keep the place spotless.

So anyway, I'm sitting here in the butty cabin staring out at what looks like the North Pole! Thank goodness we've got coal on, at least I can keep warm, even if it means we'll get a rap on the knuckles when we do deliver it. Arthur Bray's here, with Rose and Ernie, and a few Waterways pairs, so we spent last night in the White Lion, had a few beers and some music. I've told Arthur to help himself if they need any coal - they're running empty, heading for Leighton to load sand for Brentford. They've got some coal for the stoves, but if this goes on long they'll run out. I hope it soon breaks, I don't like sitting in one place!

We had a great Christmas. Mum cooked us a huge dinner, as you'd expect, and Dad had got plenty of beer in! They've got a television now, so we all watched the Queen's speech - except Dad, who fell asleep halfway through! He was so embarrassed! Gracie got the new doll's pram she wanted, and lots of other things - more toys from Mum and Dad, and two pretty dresses from James and Amanda - she's getting spoilt rotten! And so's Michael, of course, but he's too little to know much about it. I still don't quite believe it - I've got a son, Mikey. Sometimes when I look at him asleep in his pram I feel so proud I want to cry! I know it sounds silly, and I'd never say that to anyone else, but I expect you know how I feel - you must feel the same with Alby and Freddie. Daughters are lovely, but there's something special about having a son of your own, isn't there? Now I'm getting all sentimental! But I do wish, sometimes, that I could be with them all the time. But they're better off at home with Mum and Dad, it's safer for them - remember all the kids we knew who died on the boats? My brother Jack, Charlie Nixon, Nicky's brother Terry, Alice Wenlock, Freddie Bodley - when you start to think about it, the list goes on and on. And Gracie's really enjoying being at school now - she had a few days to begin with when she didn't want to go, but she soon made some friends and now she can't wait to go back after the holiday!

Did Ellie tell you we saw Joe and Grace and their children a little while ago? They all came up for a day when Nicky and I were there one Sunday before Christmas, to exchange presents and things. They're all fine, and of course it was Gabriel's birthday on Christmas Eve. Rosie's left school now, got a job for a local solicitor's office and going to secretarial college - and Jack's a fine young fellow now, tall like his granddad, and doing well at college. He's into this modern music, listens to a programme called Radio Luxembourg all the time and keeps going on about some group called the Beatles.

How's life out there in the sun? I can't imagine having Christmas in the middle of summer, it just doesn't seem right! Have the rains come now, or are you still waiting? I hope you're all okay - give our love to Carrie and tell her to write to Ellie and tell us their new address! Last we heard from them Davey and his step-dad were building the new house, but that was ages ago - have they still got just the one little boy? Tell her Josh sends his love, too. And what about Sam and Ginny, are they okay? Any sign of a little Caplin yet? Give them all our love.

Best wishes,
Steve.

January 17th 1963   Marloo Creek

Dear Ellie and Steve,

How are things going on? We've been hearing on the news here about the awful weather you've got — still no sign of a thaw? Is Stevie still on the boats, and how are you all managing? We're all worried about you — write back and keep us up to date.

We've had some rain at last, and more forecast for the next little while — the creek's running well now, and we didn't lose any cattle, although it was a close call. We're running about as many beasts as we can now, having cut right back on the sheep as the demand for wool fell off over the last few years — all this polyester and stuff has had a big effect on the wool trade here. But we're doing okay, folk will always have to eat, and beef is really in demand these days. Sam and Ginny are away for a while, taking a break down on the Sunshine Coast — they're talking about trying to start a family this year. And Carrie's doing really great.   They've moved into the new house now, and she's promised to write to you and tell you all about it.   Little Kyle's growing fast, nearly three now – and she's pregnant again.   I didn't tell you that, okay?   She'll want to break the news herself!

Our kids are all doing fine, growing like weeds – Alby's as tall as his mother now, the little rat! Twelve now – Freddie'll be nine this year – doesn't seem possible, does it? He's so brown now that Harrie had some guy in Mitchell ask if there's some blackfella in him – she soon put him right! You're right Stevie, there's something special about having boys of your own, so I know how you feel; though why you wanted to call the poor little beggar Michael I don't know!   Thanks for the pictures you sent, Ellie – but looking at the ones of him's made Harrie go all broody. We took a load of snaps over Christmas, but I haven't got the film back yet – we'll send you some when I do.   You should see our Susie now!   She's suddenly grown, got real tall and slim, and her hair's so bleached in the sun against her brown skin — she's turning into a beautiful kid, even if I say it myself. And they all talk with an Australian accent now — even I have a job understanding some of the things Freddie says when he gets excited!

We're planning a big party later this year — Jerry'll have been here for twenty years this winter, so we're going to celebrate! Harrie's in charge of the arrangements, she's going to lay on a barbie at the pub in Mitchell, and Josie Watson's going to find us a band to play for the evening. We found out a while ago that he's got a married sister living in Townsville, and Harrie managed to get in touch without him finding out — she's coming over, so as long as we can keep it all in the dark, he's got a big surprise coming! The men are all in on the secret, and they think it's a great joke, getting one over on the manager, especially the blackfellas. Sandy's habitual grin's got even wider than usual — have I told you about him before? He's been with us a few years now — looks a really fearsome fellow, black as your hat with tribal scars all over his chest, but the kids love him to pieces. He's so gentle with them, they go and sit with him in the evening sometimes and he tells them stories from the Aboriginal traditions. He comes from up in the Gulf Country originally — his wife and children were killed in some kind of racial violence about ten years ago, and he headed south, wound up with us when someone in Mitchell told him we needed more hands. I reckon he's the best horseman I know, and he's completely tireless — if he goes out to mend the fences, he's back almost before he's gone, but you know the job's been done properly.

We'll have the do in March, when the weather'll have cooled off a bit — it's real sticky here at the moment, pretty hot, and the humidity's right up with all the rain around. It makes me feel kind of nostalgic when you talk about the snow — it's funny, but for all we used to curse the cold and the damp, we do miss it somehow! It'd be nice to get up and see snow on the ground instead of just dry earth and scrub; and ice on the creek maybe — but it isn't going to happen! Tell you what, you send us some snow over and we'll send you some sunshine, melt the ice for you, how's that? It's got to break soon for you — it's been a couple of weeks now, hasn't it? Can't last much longer, then you'll be on your way again, Stevie! Anyway, take care of yourselves and say hi to everyone for us. We're thinking of you as we sit here in the sun with our cold beers!

All the best,

Mikey.

February 2nd 1963   Top Lock Cottage
                                Knowle

Hello Mikey, Harrie and the tribe,

How we're all envying you! Over a month now, and there's no sign of a let-up in this dreadful weather. We had blizzards on and off for a while - they've gone now, but it's still damned cold. Clear and bright, but it's staying below freezing even in the sunshine. The boats are still stuck at Maffers, and Nicky and I are taking turn and turn about staying on them, partly to keep them warm and stop the engine freezing up - we heard about a Willow Wren pair, stuck at Stoke Bruerne, where the water froze in the engine and split it clean in half! - and partly to make sure no-one nicks all the coal. Even the lorries are having trouble in this weather, and supplies of fuel are really sought after. It's so cold that the diesel is freezing in their pipes, and they can't get them started in the mornings - the bus service here is all over the place, doesn't run half the time because the bus engines won't go.

There's still a lot of snow about, but it's getting really dirty and slushy now.

Doesn't even look nice! The roads are mostly open again, they've done a good job clearing them but it took a while - Ellie couldn't get into town for over a week, to do any shopping or take Gracie to school, but it's okay now. And the trains are running, so I can get back and forward to the boats - Nicky's there now, but I'm going down again this weekend to relieve him. Arthur and Rose and Ernie are still there too, of course, and the BW boats.

I can't help wondering what's going to happen after this is all over. No boats can move anywhere in the country, and what loads are moving are going by lorry, or on the train. You can't expect companies to put up with getting no coal or other things they need, and if we can't take them, someone else has to - how many of them will come back to the boats, or will they decide to stick to the lorries in the future? I am worried, Mikey - but then we are better off than people like the Brays, because Ellie and I can go back on the bank and get other jobs - what will they do if the trade finishes? Blue Line 's only got two contracts as it is, and they could easily be lost after a hold-up like this - none of

83

them can read or write, so what jobs could they find? I can't imagine Ernie slaving away in some factory, and I think it would kill Arthur! You remember I told you about that church outing we did back in the summer? I can't help wondering if that's the future of the cut - we see more and more holiday boats about these days. They're a damned nuisance sometimes, hold you up at locks because they don't know what they're doing - not their fault, I suppose, but it can be frustrating when you're in a hurry. Dad said back then that we should give up carrying loads and carry people instead, and I'm beginning to think he might actually have been right, even if he did mean it as a joke!

This new bunch are running the canals now - they call themselves the British Waterways Board. Hasn't made any difference yet, but with everything frozen up there isn't much they can do! We'll wait and see if they get on with any of the maintenance that's needed, but they are doing away with the tolls! From now on, we'll pay a single yearly fee, what they're calling a license, to use the cut - it's got to be easier, for us and them - no more waiting to be gauged all over the place, and fiddling about with cash and toll tickets, and a better way for them to collect the money. Sounds really sensible - why didn't someone think of it before?

Dad's retired now, I think you knew? He soon got fed up with having nothing to do, and he's taken up making models in his spare time. He's made a lovely model of a josher motor, and now he's painting it in Fellows's colours, going to call it the Acorn, as if you couldn't guess! He was telling me that he's going to make a butty next, but he isn't sure if it'll be the Kerry, or our old Angelus. And he's doing a lot around the house now, to help Mum. That's my other worry, Mikey - she's not well, even if she won't admit it. She gets tired so quickly, has to stop and sit down all the time - it's not like her, as you will know! I've been trying to make her go and see the doctor, but she insists it's just getting old and gets all grumpy if I go on about it - and that's not like her either! There's something wrong, but until she admits it there isn't much Dad or I can do. She gets pins and needles in her hands and feet too, and I think her eyesight's going - she has to peer at things sometimes to see them properly, but again she just laughs it off if I say anything.

I spoke to Joe and Gracie on the telephone last night -- they're all fed up with this weather, like the rest of us, but making the best of it. Joe couldn't work for a few days, because their lorries wouldn't run either, but now Pickford's have got it sorted out to keep them warm enough so the engines will start in the mornings. Jack's been staying with a friend across the town so that he can get into college, and Rosie's back at work now too. Gabriel's school was closed for a bit, but it's open again now, much to his disgust! He's doing well, to be fair, enjoys most of the subjects they do, except for history and geography. Getting on well with his drama, too. He says he doesn't want to go on to college - he wants to be an engineer, so Joe's been looking around to see if there are any apprenticeships going around there. Billy's stuck at Sampson Road - they'd just unloaded steel there when the freeze came. He's getting just as frustrated as I feel, or even more so! But Sylvie's packed the children off to school while

86

they've got the chance, all except Linda of course, she's too young still.

Our Gracie's still loving school, she was quite upset when she couldn't go because of the weather, but she's happy again now! And little Michael's growing so fast - nearly five months now. He's a lovely baby, quiet and happy, not like Gracie when she was tiny, keeping us both awake half the night!

How are all your brood? Still doing okay? We had a letter from Carrie, telling us she's having another baby, and Ellie wrote back sounding all surprised. Their new house sounds grand - is it really as big as she says? And half an acre of land? But then I suppose there's plenty of that to go around in Australia, isn't there? I'm glad that you're doing so well - you're right, people will always need to eat, and what's nicer than a big juicy steak? Not that we can afford that kind of thing very often! I suppose you can have one whenever you like, with all those thousands of cattle to your name? Lucky beggar! And stop going on about how hot it is, that's really rubbing it in when we're huddled around the fire trying to keep warm!

Anyway, mate, enjoy your nice cold beer and think of us stuck here in the ice and snow. Give our love to Sam and Ginny - are they back from their holiday yet? - and to the children.

Cheers,

Steve.

February 20th 1963

Dear Steve and Ellie,

    Thanks for the letter, Steve. This cold weather must be really getting you down by now — they're still mentioning it on the radio news here from time to time. Almost two months — still no sign of a thaw? It must be some kind of record! Even in 1947, it didn't last as long as this.

    How are you managing? I know you said you've got some money coming in from the house, but things must be tight, even so. And like you said, I wonder what will happen when the weather does finally break — I remember a conversation with Harrie's Dad, a long time ago now, when he said that if there was another freeze like '47, it might well mean the end of the cut. Do you think he might have been right? We all know that the trade's been falling for years, even before we left to come here — will anyone want to use the boats after this, if they can get what they need easier and quicker by lorry? It must be very worrying for you all.

Are you serious about this idea of carrying passengers? I know you did that one trip for the church or whatever it was – but do you really think other people will want to go out on the canal like that? I can't imagine anyone actually choosing to have a trip on a boat for fun! You said something about the man who bought out Barlows having cabin cruisers that he hired out to people for holidays, too – it all sounds just ridiculous to me! I suppose, if the trade does finish, it would be a way of keeping the boats working, even if it was only an odd trip every now and then. Whatever happens, you know we all wish you well – we're thinking of you, and praying that the freeze might be over by the time you get this letter!

Have you persuaded your Mum to go to the doctor, Steve? She might be right, of course – we're all getting older, mate! Even me – it tires me out just watching Alby and

Freddie hurtling around out in the yard, now. But she ought to get a check-up, I agree with you, there might be something they could do to get her energy back — keep on at her, she'll give in eventually!

Not much changes around here. We've had a lot of rain this year, the creek broke its banks a little way up-country, flooded out our paddocks for a few days, but it soon went down again. Fortunately we'd finished shearing before it happened — we still produce quite a bit of wool, even now, although I think I've told you that we're concentrating more on the cattle now. Sam and Ginny are back now, of course — they had a great time, spent three weeks down on the Sunshine Coast, staying in Maroochydore and touring around, although Ginny was complaining that Sam spent half his time at the local boatyard, talking to the owner and helping out around the boats. It's all ocean-going cruisers and yachts, of course, not our sort of boats! But it sounds like he enjoyed himself.

Carrie and Davey are well settled in the new house now — I took a few pictures, and I'll enclose some copies for you when I send this. They send their love – her baby's due very soon, beginning of March they reckon, and Harrie is definitely getting broody! I've said that our three are quite enough to cope with, but I don't think she's convinced. Especially since Sam and Ginny are finally trying for a kid of their own! Give Josh a prod for us — his sister hasn't heard from him for ages!

The planning for Jerry's party is well under way here — and he still doesn't know anything about it! March 24th is the day we've set for it; we're having a big barbie in Mitchell, with music laid on.

Well, there isn't much else to tell you — Harrie and the kids all send their love. I'll write to your Mum and Dad, Steve, see if I can't help to get her to see a doctor. Give them our love anyway, and to everyone else.

Best wishes,
Mikey.

March 2nd 1963

Dear Mikey, Harrie and tribe,

Thanks for your letter, and the photos. The kids all look so wonderfully brown and healthy – you all do, come to that! I showed them to Vi, and she says that Alby looks just like you when they first found you, even if he's got a better suntan. And Susie really is getting to be a lovely girl – you'll have all the local boys after her in a few years time! And Freddie looks like a real sweetie – isn't he like his Mum?

Carrie's new house looks very grand – did they really build it all themselves? And she's looking very well, if a bit bulgy! Her Davey is a handsome lad, too, and Little Kyle looks like the spitting image of him. I suppose your winter is coming on now – we do feel sorry for you! All those dry, bright, warm days, and clear nights, while here we are luxuriating in the snow and the ice, with nice cold gales to keep us on our toes... By the way, Josh has promised to write to Carrie, very soon – believe it if you will!

The weather here hasn't changed, as you may have gathered. Everything is still frozen, and even the weather men on the radio can't say if or when it's going to end. It has too, soon, surely? It'll be spring in a few weeks, so it must start to warm up then – I hope! Stevie is down on the boats at the moment, and

I'm sure he'll write to you when he gets back here after the weekend, but I thought I'd drop you a quick line anyway.

Everyone here is well, as far as I know. Bill seems to be enjoying his retirement, spends a lot of time in his little workshop – Steve told you he's taken up making model boats, didn't he? Gracie's still enjoying school, doing well there – and Michael's growing like a weed! Mum says he looks like me, but he's definitely got his Daddie's eyes. Jimmy's doing well up in Sheffield, got himself a regular girlfriend now – Joe and Grace were fine, the last we heard from them. Billy's still stuck, of course, fuming quietly, as you'll imagine! But he's found some temporary work in Birmingham, and the kids are all going to the local school – I know Sylvie's pleased about that! The only one not so good is Vi – I know Stevie's told you that he's worried about her. She isn't right, we can all see that, but will she admit there's anything wrong? She gets so tired – and her eyesight is definitely giving her trouble, but she just laughs it off as old age if we say anything. Yes, please, Mikey – write to her and try and make her see sense, if you haven't already! She still thinks the world of you, and she might just take notice if you suggest she sees the doctor.

Well, there's not much else to tell you, I think.
Take care of yourselves – and wrap up warm through
that awful winter, try to keep the beer nice and cold!
All our love,
Ellie.

March 5th 1963

Dear Mikey, Harriet, Alby, Susie, Freddie;

Thanks for the letter. Ellie says she's already written back to you with the 'home' news. And thanks for the pictures, it's nice to see how you're all looking these days, even if we're green with envy at all that sunshine! Mum says Alby's getting to look just like you as a boy, and I can see what she means. Poor little beggar!

Nothing's changed here, we're still frozen up solid. Other things are working almost as normal, despite the freeze - the trains are running even if the timetable's a bit hit-and-miss, and the roads are mostly okay now. But the cut's still completely at a standstill, nothing moving at all. They kept the channel open in Birnigum for a while when it first froze, but even they had to give up when it went on and on. Our boats are still okay - Nicky's there now, but I'm going back down in a few days, as he's managed to get some casual work with a local garage in Harefield, where Jack and Maggie are living now.

Thanks for your concern about our finances! As you say, it's not too bad, with the rent money from the house, and I've been doing a bit for the Waterways while I'm down at Maffers - you remember there's the maintenance yard there? Arthur Bray and Ernie have been working for them on and off, too, so they're not as badly placed as they might have been - and we've got plenty of coal left, so far! I've had to help myself from the load, but it's only been a few bucket fulls, and I've given a bit to Arthur for their ranges, too. I suppose there'll be an inquest when we finally get to Nash Mills! But I'm not sure I care - what else are we supposed to do, freeze to death? Remember the Beecheys, back in 1947 - that was tragic, wasn't it?

And I'm really thinking about what we're going to do after all this. Can the cut go on, will there be any trade at all, or will it all go to the roads and the trains? I'm quite tempted to try Dad's suggestion, and put an ad in the local papers at home, see if there are people who would want to hire the boats for a day out. If we carry on as we are, assuming there's some loads to be had, and try and get a bit of passenger work as well - I'm not sure if it'll work, but it can't hurt to try. What do you think, Mikey? We'll be down to Bulls Bridge after Nash Mills, of course, so I'll try and find out from them how things are likely to go in the future.

It sounds as though you're looking forward to the winter - it must be a relief from all that heat! You can have ours, if you want it, mate! It would be wonderful to feel warm again - we're all right at home, of course, but it would be great to see the back of the ice and feel the sun on our faces again.

Well, not much else to tell you, I suppose. Oh - Ellie's just reminded me - we heard from Grace the other day, it seems Rosie came a cropper off her bike on the way to college in the week. She's not too bad, broke her arm and got a bit knocked about, but they say she'll be fine in a week or two. Apparently Jack's teasing her unmercifully now, but Grace says he was really upset and worried when it first happened - he likes to play the tough jack-the-lad, but he's a bit of a softy underneath, she reckons! And Joe's got an apprenticeship lined up for Gabriel, when he leaves school, with a local engineering firm.

And, while I think of it - you know Josh finished his apprenticeship? Now he's earning some decent money, he and Laura are talking about getting married. Don't know when yet - we'll let you know! I guess that's why he's been so preoccupied lately.

That really is all for now. Take care of yourselves, and give our love to Sam and Ginny, tell them we're waiting to hear about a little Caplin very soon!

All the best,

Steve.

March 14th 1963   Bull's Bridge Depot

Hello everyone!

Just a quick letter to let you know that the big freeze is over at last! I guess this might well cross with a letter from you, but I wanted to bring you up to date with things.

It was two days ago, on the 12th - the weather changed suddenly, overnight. Heavy clouds, and lots of rain. Everything thawed very quickly, and with the rain as well, there were floods everywhere, still are in lots of places. The cut was pretty well swamped, but we got away yesterday, and made it to Nash Mills and unloaded this morning. We're at Bulls Bridge now - missed the office, so I'll go and talk to them in the morning.

To be honest, I don't know what to expect. A lot of loads must have been lost to the lorries and trains, for all time, so even if there is still some trade on the cut I doubt if Waterways will have any use for outside contractors like us any more - they'll have trouble finding enough work for their own boats, I reckon. And I've got another problem – Nicky wants to leave. He was working part-time in that garage in Harefield, during the freeze, and they obviously liked him because they've offered him a full-time job, and to train him as a proper mechanic. He really wants to go, but he's feeling guilty about leaving me with the boats – I've told him that he's got to take it up. Even if we can keep on working, how long is it going to last? He'd be stupid not to take the chance to move on to a job that's likely to keep him working for the rest of his life, rather than stay here out of some sense of loyalty just to end up out of work in the end! I've asked him to help me get the boats back to Dad's house at Knowle, but told him after that to go home and start this new job. I hope he does well; he's a really nice lad, and deserves a good life.

I'll see what the office has to say tomorrow, and then decide what to do. I could probably get another mate, if I need to, there'll be enough redundant boaters around I imagine! Or if we just use the boats for passengers, Ellie and I can do that, day by day – or if she wants to stay at home with the kids, I expect Dad would stand in. I think we'll try that ad in the papers, anyway, just to see!

That's it for now! Sighs of relief all round, as you can imagine. We'll write again soon, with a bit more news;

Best wishes,

Steve.

March 25th 1963

Dear Steve and Ellie,

  I'd started to write back to you when we got the news over the radio that your great freeze had ended at last! I hung on then, knowing that you'd have written again – thanks for the letters! We're all so pleased that things are on the move again for you, but we know what you mean about the doubts for the future. What did Waterways say, Steve, are there any loads to be had now? Let us know – we're all on tenterhooks, wondering what will happen.

  I still can't quite make out this idea of holidays on the cut – it seems so strange, like going on a train just for the sake of the trip rather than to get somewhere. But if as you say other people are doing it, hiring boats out, then I suppose there must be people who want them! And there was that fellow Nicholl, bought the old Arcturus and started doing trips down in Cassio Park, wasn't there? He was at it even when we were still on the cut. And I seem to remember hearing that someone had bought Fellows's old Linda, to do the same thing — was that right? What happened to them, do you know? If they're doing all right, maybe you could do the same, have the Albert converted for passengers! It would be easier to have just the motor, rather than trying to run a pair — like you say, you and Ellie, or your Dad, could do that, but you'd need more if you used the butty too. And you'd have to have someone to look after the passengers, wouldn't you?

I did write to your parents, Steve, and tried (diplomatically!) to suggest your Mum sees the doctor. Don't know if she'll take any notice of me — she never has before! I hope she's all right. And how's Rosie now? Give her our best wishes if you're speaking to them any time — I have written to Joe and Grace anyway.

Lots happening here, lately! We had Jerry's bash yesterday, went off a treat — plenty of beer, a great barbie at the pub, everyone had a grand time. You should have seen his face when his sister walked in — they haven't met for about ten years, and it was really emotional. I declared a day off today — everyone's too hung over to do much, as I expected! And Carrie's baby was born on the 15th — a bit late, but they're both fine. Another boy — they're going to call him Todd. Little Kyle seems overjoyed at the idea of a little brother. Harrie keeps dropping hints about us having another kid — I'm not convinced, but I suppose there's no reason why we couldn't. We can certainly afford it — and it would make her so happy. The other kids have got wind of the idea — Susie and Freddie are all for it, but Alby seems kind of doubtful, I'm not sure why! I'll keep you posted.

They had a real wet summer up in the north of Queensland this year, floods everywhere, but the worst of it didn't reach us although we did have a bit of a go for a while. Down south, where it's much drier this time of year, they had a real bad bush fire around Melbourne way. This is a crazy country, but we wouldn't swap it for anywhere else now! Even if it would be nice just to see some snow again, one day.

Not much else to tell you right now. Take care of yourselves, and give our love to everyone — write back and let us know how things are, what your plans are for the future.

Cheers,
Mikey.

April 8th 1963   Top Lock Cottage
                                     Knowle

Dear Mikey, Harrie and crew,

Thanks for the letter, Mikey. We had a note from Carrie as well, telling us about the baby - she sounds so happy with life! How are Sam and Ginny getting on? And we're pleased that your big celebration went off well - you all deserve it, not just Jerry! It sounds as though you have a real good team working for you out there.

As for us back here - I'm not sure if I'm depressed or hopeful, to be honest! I know that sounds silly. The cut's about finished, Mikey, at least as we knew it. Waterways have given up - there's no more carrying fleet! When I got to the office at Bulls Bridge, the manager there just told me to go home; I gather all their own crews were told the same. A few smaller companies are trying to go on - Willow Wren have got money troubles, but Leslie Morton's trying to hold it together, keep the few contracts they've still got running, and there are one or two independent carriers still going. Blue Line are still there, but I think they've lost the sand traffic - just doing the coal run to the Jam 'Ole now. Three pairs - Brays, Whitlocks and Collins's. It's so sad, after all these years - so many good people with no work, with their whole life finished, really. Billy's furious, as you can imagine! But he's resigned to it now. They're still living in the boat, tied in Sampson Road, and he's managed to get part-time work for a local builder. Sylvie's got the children accepted full-time in the school there, and she's helping out with the school dinners, leaving little Linda with one of the other boat-women there - she's four now, goes to school herself this year! Emmie's fourteen next month - it's scary how time goes by, isn't it?

But looking on the positive side - I went to see Bryan Nicholl down at Cassio after we got the boats back here. Like you, I thought of him - we'd seen the boat about, full of people a lot of the time, so he seemed like a good fellow to talk to. He's given me a lot of good advice. I'd forgotten about the Linda, but you're right - it's running at Foxton, on the Leicester line, belongs to a fellow called Crossley, and I'm going to get in touch with him too and see what he thinks of the passenger business! Dad and I are thinking about doing just what you said, Mikey - putting a canopy on the Albert, maybe a little bar where we could sell beer and soft drinks. We should be able to get fifty or sixty people on board at a time, and if we did trips up towards Katie de Barnes or down towards Hatton, even at a couple of bob a time, we ought to make enough. We're not far from Solihull and the edge of Birnigum, and even Coventry, so we're going to advertise in those areas.

Dad's all for it - I think because he can't wait to get back on a boat! And James is going to help us all he can - he's said he'll build the canopy and put a false floor in the boat's bottom for us, so people can see over the side. And while we get things going, I'm going to go back to work for him in the week, so we'll have money coming in. All in all, everything's looking good - but we all know it's a bit of a gamble! We're going to repaint the boat too - I want to keep your old red and white colours, but it makes sense to advertise on the cabinsides. I hope you don't mind?

That's all of our plans - I'll let you know as things go on.

I'm in trouble with Ellie now, because I've just gone on and on about the boats! She's going to take over and bring you up to date on the family stuff.

Steve.

Hello, Mike, Harrie and all!

If I left it to Stevie, you'd never get to know anything about the rest of us! Gracie's fine, still enjoying going to school – six now, we had her birthday party in January, of course. And Michael's growing day by day – seven months old next week!

Thanks for the letter you wrote to Steve's Mum and Dad, Mikey – Vi's still baulking at the idea of going to the doctor, says it's a waste of his time, she's only getting old, but I think what you said has made her think about it. Maybe we'll get her there in the end. Bill's as fit and strong as ever, and as Stevie says, he's itching to get on the boat again! My Dad's going to start on the conversion as soon as he's finished a job he's on at the moment, and we're hoping to be ready for business before the summer comes. Now I'm talking about the damned boats, too!

Josh has moved out, living with Laura's parents in Tilehouse Green – the wedding's supposed to be next year, he tells us! We all miss him, but it does leave the rest of us a bit more room here!

I had a long chat with Grace on the phone the other day – they're all okay, Rosie soon got over her tumble from the bike, and she's back at work now. Jack's studying hard, doing well – eighteen next month, how is it possible? And Gabriel can't wait to leave school and start his apprenticeship, but he's got another year to go yet! Although he's got into a theatrical agency too, really enjoying his acting – he's even had a few little walk-on parts on television recently. She did say that Joe's Dad isn't too good, apparently his back is really bad now and he's pretty well stuck in his wheelchair – have you heard from them recently?

My parents are both well, and Jimmy sends his love – he and Pat are thinking of getting married, maybe next year, if his job goes well. They want to buy their own house, and I'm sure Dad will help them out if they do! Stevie's told you about Billy and Sylvie – they're all well, the older kids getting on well in school thanks to Sylv's teaching while they were boating!

Carrie seems to be really happy, from the note she sent us – send us some pictures of them and the new baby, if you can, we'd love to see them. And give them our love – I'll write myself in the next day or two. Are you two going to try for another baby? Why not – you've got three lovely kids, but you're still young enough to cope with another one! And give our best wishes to Sam and Ginny!

Well, I think that's about all for now. Stevie will no doubt be writing again as things progress on the boat! In the meantime, look after yourselves.

With our love,

Ellie.

April 25th 1963

Hi all!

Don't know if you've written since our last to you, but I had to drop you a line. You should see the Albert now! Or maybe you shouldn't - it looks a lot different. We've got a full-length canopy from the front of the engine-hole to the fore-end, which finishes directly above the deck-beam, on a light wooden frame. The front part is made of canvas, so it'll roll back in the better weather, and the back half is quarter-inch plywood, all thoroughly soaked in creosote so it should last okay and not go rotten. There're roll-down windows along the back half, so we can keep the passengers dry if it rains, too. James and I built most of it over a couple of weekends, and Dad helped out a lot too. And he's repainted the cabinsides in your old colours, and we're getting them signwritten next week. James and I are going to put seats in, fixed all around both sides, and we've started on fitting a kind of false floor eighteen inches above the shuts. Everyone's getting quite excited about the whole thing!

But the best thing is - I put some adverts in the Solihull papers, to see what would happen, and we've had a flood of enquiries! Well, maybe that's being a bit optimistic, but there've been enough people ringing up about it to make me think we really could do quite well once we're actually in operation. We've taken names and phone numbers, and explained to the people that the boat isn't quite ready, and they seem happy to wait.

We have to have a license from the Board of Trade to run as a passenger boat - something that Bryan Nicholl told me about. The man from the Ministry came yesterday, and went over the boat - he seems quite happy, and says they'll send me the certificate in the next few days. So we're nearly ready to go! I know it's a huge change from what we've always done, but if it means we can keep boating, and that the cut itself will go on, then it's got to be worth it, don't you think? I know there's still some carrying going on, but honestly Mikey, I don't know how long it can last.

I feel kind of guilty sometimes, as though I'm giving up on our way of life - but where's the sense in trying to go on and on if it's all going to finish anyway? I hope what we're doing will keep at least some boats working even if it is in a very different way - and I hope you approve of it? We owe you so much for the opportunity to go back on the cut, I hope you don't think we're just copping out?

Anyway, do write back soon. Love to Harrie and the kids, and to Sam and Ginny, and Carrie and her family. Josh has promised he's going to write to her - again!

All the best,

Steve.

May 15th 1963

Dear Steve and Ellie,

Thanks for the latest update on progress! It seem strange to picture the old boat with a canopy, and seats and a bar — I imagine it looking a lot like the Arcturus when we used to see it around Cassio those last few years we were on the cut? I'm pleased you've kept the same colours, but of course you need to have the signwriting advertising your new trade! Don't feel guilty about that. I suppose I do feel rather sad, knowing that our old way of life is all over — I know it was hard at times, but we had so many good times too, didn't we? And it saved my life — if you and your family hadn't been there that night, I would have died, and look what I would be missing now!

I'm sure you've made the right decision, Stevie. Henry was right, wasn't he? Another big freeze-up, and the trade's all finished — like you, I can't see the few boats that are left going on much longer, the lorries are so much faster, and if they're anything like the ones we have here, they're getting bigger and bigger as time goes by. Before long, they'll be carrying as much as a pair of boats! And no hold-ups because of ice. Out here, they sometimes get stuck in the summer rains when the roads flood, but you don't have that trouble, do you?

And it means you'll be able to be at home all the time, with Ellie and the kids — that must mean a lot to you. Will you work for James when the boat isn't out? You'll be earning more than us at this rate!

Life here's back to normal now — winter's coming on, so it's nice and cool. We actually had a frost on the ground the other morning, unusual at this time of year — it's usually later, around July, we see that — and the days are bright and clear. Harrie and I are taking the kids away for a couple of weeks, having a break. Sam and Ginny will be here, with Jerry of course, to run the place. We're going to Maroochydore, where they stayed after Christmas, going to explore the coast and all around – they were so full of it after their holiday! And it's the first time we've had a real holiday ourselves – we've been away for the odd few days, but this will be a real rest, two weeks away, new places, new people – the gang at home are great, and the folks in Mitchell, but it will be nice to see new faces! And it'll give Harrie and I time to talk – we're seriously thinking about trying for another baby. I'm 35 now, and Harrie will be in a few months time, so we can't wait too much longer if we're going to. Another few years, maybe – and they say it's more risky as the mother gets older, don't they? Susie's all for it, and I think Freddie's got ideas of a little brother to play with! Alby just kind of shrugs the idea off – he'll be 13 soon, and I suppose babies aren't a thing to get excited about if you're a teenage boy! I think he's a bit afraid a new baby will distract us too much – me especially, he and I spend a lot of time together nowadays, out about the station.

He's a terrific rider, much better on a horse than me — you should see him when we go on muster, rounding up the cattle! He and Sandy, the big Blackfella, work together a lot, and it's like a work of art watching them herding a big mob into the paddocks. I'm so proud of him — of Susie and Freddie too of course, but he's my oldest son, and to see him growing into a fine young man just makes my heart sing. And if you ever tell him that I'll strangle you!

How are everyone at home? Give them all our love. How's your Mum, Stevie, has she seen the doctor yet? Take care of yourselves, and the very best of luck with your new project!

Best wishes,

Mikey.

June 3rd 1963

Hello Mikey, Harrie and all!

How are things with you - I hope you had a great holiday? Back to the day job now, I expect! Any news about another baby - Ellie's itching to know!

We're doing fine - the kids are great, Gracie loving school and Michael growing like a weed. The only worry is Mum - she still won't see the doctor, but we're working on her. I know Dad's worried, even if he doesn't say anything.

I know you've always been doubtful about the business of holiday boats on the cut, Mikey - you wouldn't believe what we've been doing! The Albert was ready for work at the beginning of May, and we were out every Saturday and Sunday with different groups of people from the towns around here! They're queueing up to come for a trip with us - even I can't believe it! Over the Whitsun weekend, we didn't take bookings but advertised in the papers for people to just come along on the day - and we didn't stop! The weather was good, dry and mostly sunny, and we ran from the top of the locks here to the winding hole at Henwood Bridge, just short of Katie de Barnes - you know where I mean? About an hour round trip, and we had a queue waiting every time, didn't stop until six o'clock every day.

Dad and I take turns steering and looking after the passengers - you should have seen the look on his face as he set off on his first trip! Like a kid at Christmas, he was! And the passengers love talking to him - they get him on the old days, when he was a kid on Grandad's horse-boat, and they just lap it up. And while they're talking to him, they keep on buying drinks too! We've got a little bar just in front of the engine-hole, where we sell bottles of beer and soft drinks for the kids, and packets of crisps - helps to make a bit more money as well as keeping people happy!

I know it's sad to see the end of our old life, Mikey, but we've got to face facts - it's all but finished anyway. And this has to be the future of the cut - passengers, and holiday boats. It's difficult to know how much of the cut will survive, though - so much is in an awful state, sludged up so that you can't get around, the locks barely workable. But there are people trying to do things about that - there's a bunch calling themselves the Inland Waterways Association, campaigning against the government to save the canals. And another lot, led by a fellow called David Hutchings, who are actively trying to reopen the old Stratford cut, digging the mud out and fixing the locks and everything! Charlie Crossley's just taken the Linda over there, running trips on the length around Wootton Wawen to support their efforts to get it all reopened, at least down to Stratford on Avon.

We're all right around here - there's still some traffic coming this way, and the loaded boats keep a good channel clear. And if things go on the way they've started, we're going to have no trouble making a decent living! I'm earning more than I ever could carrying, and it's so nice to see the smiles on people's faces when they get off the boat after a trip - so different from dealing with the miserable beggars at Brentford docks or around the wharves in Birnigum! And of course I'm at home with

Ellie and the kids, and that means a lot, especially now that Gracie's growing up.

I'd better close - got paperwork to do! I have to keep up-to-date records, of course, for the tax people and so on, and it's best not to let it get behind! James has run his own business for a long time now, and he's been so helpful with advice as well as converting the boat.

Everyone here sends their love - take care of yourselves, and keep in touch.

Steve.

Interlude

1964

November 27th 1964   Top Lock Cottage
                      Knowle

Dear Mike and all,

I don't know if you got the telegram we sent yesterday - don't know how well things like that get through to you out there in the wilds. In case you didn't - the bad news is that we lost my Mum the day before yesterday.

You know how worried we'd all been about her, for so long now - she'd still never seen the doctor, and now it's too late. Dad and I were out on the boat with a party from the local school - when we got back, he found her in the kitchen. She'd collapsed, in the middle of cooking the dinner for us, the stew was still bubbling on the stove - Ellie and the kids were going to come over and join us all later. We called the ambulance and they rushed her into hospital, but she died that night.

Perhaps the worst part of it was having to ring Josh and tell him. You know how devoted he's always been to her, since she took him in after the accident at

Limehouse Dock - the poor kid tried to hold it in, but he broke down on the phone, and Laura had to take over. He wants to come and see her at the mortuary - I'm not sure it's a good idea, but he's insistent. I suppose you can understand!

They'll have to have an inquest, because she died suddenly, but the doctor there says she almost certainly had something they call diabetes. It's something that goes wrong sometimes as you get older, and means that you can't digest sugar properly - he says it would account for how tired she got, and the pins and needles and her poor eyesight, and everything. If only she'd seen a doctor, it might have been controlled - they can't cure it, but he says that you can help by changing your diet and things like that.

But there you are - you know what she was like, Mikey. She'd made up her mind it was just old age, and nothing was going to change her. Dad's devastated, as you can imagine - he's keeping up appearances as best he can, especially in front of the kids, but underneath he's quite lost without her. I spoke to Ellie and James yesterday - we're going to talk to Waterways, see if we can buy their house or lease it so he doesn't have to move - if we can buy it, James and I might extend it, and then Ellie and I could move in with him. He'd have company, and we'd be on the spot for the business, so it would make a lot of sense.

The business has been going very well - we're so busy you can't imagine! Dad and I were talking about getting a couple of boats we could hire out for holidays, like Michael Streat at Braunston - he's doing very well at it, and it would be another string to our bow, so to speak. Maybe once Mum's buried we'll take up the idea - it'll be something to help him get over it, perhaps.

We don't know when the funeral will be yet, because of the inquest. And you will be just coming up to shearing now, won't you? A busy time, I guess - If you can't make it back, Mikey, don't worry or feel guilty. Mum would have been the first to tell you to look after your own lives rather than worry about her - and you don't need the expense, I'm sure, especially after Harriet and Sam flying back for Henry's funeral just a few months ago. And you've got baby Anna to look after too, now. We'll give her a good send-off, don't worry about that! And she'll know that you're thinking about her, sitting up there on her little cloud keeping an eye on us all!

Sorry to send such sad news - we all send our love too.

Steve.

Part Three

1969

October 13th 1969   Top Lock House
                                     Knowle

Dear Mike, Harrie and the kids

     Thanks for your last letter, and the new
pictures. It's difficult to believe how the children have
all grown up so much — Alby looks a fine young
man, completely at home on the back of that
enormous horse! Is he really nineteen now — I suppose
he must be! And Susie — she's a real beauty, you
must be so proud of her — I'll bet the local boys are all
after her! Freddie - can he be fifteen, when I still
remember him as the little toddler he was when you
left England? And Anna looks like a cute kid too,
five now?

     How is business these days, now you don't
have Sam and Ginny there with you? I suppose
Alby's taking on a lot more now that he's finished
college, and I know you've always said that Jerry
really runs the place! How are Sam and Ginny —
settling in to life on the coast? I'll drop them a line
when I've finished this letter. I suppose you can
understand Sam's decision — Marloo Creek has
always really been your place, and the opportunity to
go and play with boats again must have been too
good to resist! It's such a shame that they can't have

children – is it definite, or is there anything the doctors can do about it? I feel so sorry for Ginny especially, and it makes me realize how lucky I am to have Gracie and Michael. They're both fine, and doing well in school.

It's going to be all change here for us too, this winter. We're going to become a limited company! It doesn't seem possible, does it? Stevie as a managing director! Not bad for an 'illiterate bargee', as that awful bank manager called him just a few years ago! We've come so far in just those few years too – from the first two old cabin cruisers he bought just after Vi died, to a fleet of eight boats now as well as the Albert, still going strong and making money from the passenger trips. Steve says he's going to write to you soon, and tell you all about his plans, so I won't say too much now.

I took the kids over to see Joe and Grace last weekend – they're both very well, getting used to a quiet house again now! Jack's doing well for himself, apparently, away in America at the moment working on some kind of exchange deal. Rosie's settling in to married life – her Robert seems like a really nice fellow, and I gather he's regarded as a top man in his office. He's a solicitor, but I expect you knew that? She met him at work. Only Gabriel's at home now, and that only when he's between jobs! He's really making a name for himself – we see him on the television from time to time, and Grace was telling us he's been offered a part in a big film which they're going to make at Elstree Studios very soon. Twenty-one in December!

Billy and Sylvie are fine too – you know they're living in our old house in Knowle? Billy's settled down as he's got older – thank goodness! Emily's twenty now, studying hard at Aston University in Birmingham, and Bill Junior's finished his A-levels, taking a year out to help his Dad and Stevie re-organising the business before he goes off to college. Violet's a pretty girl, fifteen now! She's not exactly academic, bless her, but she's an amazing athlete, wins cups all over the place for her swimming. She wants to be a PE teacher when she's older. And Linda's just started at senior school of course – eleven last month!

My little (!) brother and his wife finally emigrated to Canada in June – we've had a couple of letters, and it seems they're really loving it out there. It seems as if everyone's emigrating these days – have you seen anything of Josh and Laura since they move d to Melbourne? My Dad's still working as hard as ever – the building trade doesn't ever seem to let up – and Mum's well. They both send their love. And Steve's Dad is really fine now – the trip-boating with the Albert has become very much his baby, and he's loving every minute of it! The old part of the house by the canal is his domain, and Stevie and I and the kids live in the new part which we built on the back, so we can all be private or together as a family depending on how we feel — it works very well for all of us.

Well, I guess that's about all the family news from this end. Do write back soon — it's always good to hear from you all. Give our love to your kids, and to Carrie and Davey and their tribe, and Sam and Ginny of course. Take care of yourselves.

All our love

Ellie.

October 28th 1969   Marloo Creek Stn
                                Qld.

Dear Steve & Ellie,

Thanks for your letter, Ellie, and the family round-up! It's good to have news of them all, and to know everything's going well back there in the Old Country. We haven't heard from Stevie yet — if he hasn't written, give him a good hard nudge will you? The plans for the business sound really exciting — I knew things had been going well, but this sounds like a real big step forward and I'm dying to know all about it.

As you say, things here are a lot different now too. It seemed very strange at first, not having Sam and Ginny living next door, having him by my side all the time around the property — but you are quite right when you say that although he was a great help, there really isn't enough to keep both of us busy here, at least for large parts of the year. And the offer he had to go and work on the Sunshine Coast was almost too good to be true! He's always had the knack of working on engines, and he'd been spending half his time at that boatyard helping out whenever they've been there on 'holiday', much to Ginny's disgust! What they've offered him is effectively to have his own business, subbing to them whenever they need him but free to do whatever other work he can get — and as you said, he's playing with boats again, even if they are very different from our old narrowboats! Not much opportunity for that here in the bush! The coast all along there is so lovely too — it'll be a great place for them to live, and I know Ginny wants them to get a boat of their own right away so they can enjoy it at its best. We're all on a promise to go and stay with them any time, and that'll be fair dinkum, you can imagine! Freddie's itching to go and try his hand at sea-fishing with them, and we've kind of promised that if they're settled in their own house by then, we'll go and have Christmas with them.

We'll be coming up to shearing end of next month, and it'll be the first time without them here — but we've been running the mobs down over the last few years anyway, with the drop in the price of wool, so it won't be a problem. I'll miss having Sam here to help, though, and of course I miss my little sister! Ginny still owns half of Marloo Creek, of course — the place was left to both of us, as you'll remember, and we've agreed that I'll pay her a dividend from the profits every year although most of it will go back into the business, as ever.

Jerry is still the manager here, you're right — and he's still the expert! We all defer to him when it comes to the animals and the running of the place, even if I guess I know pretty well as much as he does after all these years of working with him. He's been a great teacher as well as the best manager I could have wished for — other properties have tried to poach him from me a couple of times, but he's always turned them down, bless him! He's been brilliant with the kids all this time as well, treating them almost like they were his own, and they've all adopted him as a kind of stand-in Grandad — I wonder sometimes if it's his affection for them that's kept him here rather than working for me! And over the last few years he's been actively training Alby to take over as manager — Jerry must be well over sixty now, although he won't admit how old he really is!

Alby made up his mind a long time ago, when he was about thirteen, that he was going to run Marloo Creek one day, and of course it will be his inheritance along with his brother and sisters. He's been studying agriculture and husbandry at college, and I guess he knows more than me about the business now! At least the theory of it all. He's an amazing young man — I can't call him a kid any more — and you're right, I'm so proud of him. Watching him on a horse, bringing in the mobs or rounding up the cattle, I can't sometimes believe that he's really my son, my boy. Just to have him at my side as we ride out from the sheds, my heart feels ready to burst — you'll know what I mean, I'm sure, Steve. And if you ever let on to him I'll come over there and bloody-well shoot you!

The other kids are all wonderful, of course, but Alby's my oldest — you understand. Yes, Susie's a lovely girl — good thing she takes after her mother! — and she's almost as good around the property as Alby, probably rides better than he does, if I'm honest. Freddie's a great kid — studying hard, bless him, he's still determined he wants to be a doctor, work for the RFDS, but whether he'll get the grades to take him there I don't know. It won't be for the want of trying, though! And little Anna — what can I say? I'm so pleased now that I let Harrie persuade me to have another child, she's really brought a new sun into our lives since she's been around. She's such a happy kid, all the time, brown as a button even if she's got my blond hair, a real outback tomboy!

We were at the pub in Mitchell the other day, and Carrie and Davey send their love to you all — they've taken over running the place now, did we tell you? Davey's Mum, Josie, lost her husband a couple of years back, and she decided to give it away last summer. She still owns the place, but Davey and Carrie are managing it for her while she enjoys her retirement! They're loving it — Carrie still surprises us, after the years when she was so withdrawn, after Charlie Nixon was killed, she's changed so completely. She really loves the company and the bustle of the pub, runs the bar there like she was born to it, doesn't take any nonsense from anyone, even the toughest swaggie! Davey looks after the business side of things, keeps more in the background, but he's devoted to her and the boys. They're growing up, now — Kyle's just turned eight, and Todd's six. Harrie was asking if they want any more kids, and I think they might in a year or two once they've got used to the life at the pub. We have seen Josh and

Laura once, they took a trip to Brisbane and we went in to meet them, Carrie too — it was quite an emotional reunion, we can imagine! They seem to have settled in all right, renting a house in Glen Iris.

Sam's been on the phone since I started writing to you — they've found the house they want, down the coast a way in Alexandra Headland. It's not cheap, that's a pricey area, but it sounds great — and the business here can afford to lend them the money to buy. So it sounds like Christmas here we come!

Anyway, I guess that's about all of our news for now. Do write and let us know all about the plans you have, Steve — we're all thinking of you, rooting for you all the way!

All the best

Mike and Harrie.

November 15th 1969   Top Lock Cottage
                       Knowle

Hi Mikey, Harriet and all!

Sorry I haven't written before, Ellie's been on my case to drop you a line for ever! But there's been so much to do, so much to think about.

If I stop to think about it, I find it hard to believe where we've got to, in such a short time. That decision, after Mum died, to buy those two old cabin cruisers and try hiring them out to people for their holidays was the best thing I've ever done - even if I wasn't too sure about it at the time. To be honest, it was almost as much a way of trying to help Dad get over her loss as anything else, to keep us both occupied - but look how it's paid off!

Two more old boats the following year, and people queueing up to hire them out - we've got eight now, as you know, and I reckon we could probably use twice as many if we had them. It was James, who's been such a great help all along, who said it was time we set it all up as a 'proper' company, and I know he's right.

143

So as of the beginning of next year, we'll be 'Midland Canal Holidays Ltd' - how about that? What a way to start the new decade!

I'll be in charge - managing director, they call it. One in the eye for that manager at the old bank who didn't want to know about us back when we first started! The man at the bank we use now couldn't be better, or more helpful - I think he can see where his bread's buttered! They're lending us enough to buy our first two new boats, proper narrowboats this time - they're going to be built at Braunston, by Braunston Boats. The design is by a fellow called Chris Barney, and they'll sleep four or five people - just right for a family holiday, so we're hoping they'll be really popular. They'll have steel hulls and wood cabins - they build them with a skin of fabric coated with a kind of resin outside, which makes them really weatherproof, and nice little two-cylinder engines mounted at the back, under the step where you steer. I've had the chance to try one out, and they handle really well - not like a full-length boat of course, but pretty neat and nippy - and you can turn them around almost anywhere, because they're only 45 feet long!

Ellie is going to be what they call the company secretary, and look after the books and all that kind of thing - not my scene, as you'll understand! Thanks to you, Mikey, I can read and write quite well, but she's the scholard! And Dad's going to be another director - he's chuffed to bits, grinning from ear to ear. He's pretty much taken over running the old Albert now, and still loving it - we get all kinds of trips on it, from local schools to W I groups and everything in between. James will be a director too, but only as a kind of sleeping partner - he has his own business of course, but his help and advice has been so important all the way along, and I hope will be in the future too.

And Billy's working with us too. He and Sylv have moved into our old house, buying it off of us, and he's going to take care of the day-to-day running of the boats, the maintenance and all that kind of thing. Young Bill is taking a year out - he's off to college after that, to study Chemistry - so that he can work for us too while we're getting it all set up through next year. I think it'll be useful for him, give him an idea of what life's all about rather than drifting off to college with his head in the clouds!

So yes, my old friend, lots of changes back here in grotty, grey old England! It's raining out there today - winter's well on its way, but we're all looking forward to next spring and the launch of our new boats and the new business. It seems so long ago that we were all on the boats together, Mikey - we heard the other day that the wheat contract's finished, no more boats going down the Wellingborough river. As far as I know, only Blue Line are still going, and then they've only got the Jam 'Ole contract, carrying coal from up the Coventry cut to Southall.

Ellie and the kids send their love, as does Dad. Say Hi to Sam and Ginny for us, and to Carrie and her family, wish them well with the pub. And tell Harrie to send us a picture of the two of you sometime, not just the kids - Michael keeps asking what his 'Uncle Mike' looks like!

With all our best wishes,
Steve.

December 18th 1969

Hi Steve, Ellie;

Sorry I haven't written before — you know we've been shearing the last week or two, a real busy time for us. And we've had a nasty time of it — Susie had a real bad accident. Don't worry, she's going to be okay, but it'll take a while — she's feeling pretty crook right now, mostly I think because she's blaming herself for what happened.

It wasn't her fault, that I'm sure, even if we don't really know what did happen. She was out with Jerry and some of the boys bringing in a mob from right out west. Jerry says something spooked her horse — she loves to ride this big black stallion, Rocket. He's big brute, very strong and very fast — anyway, something made him rear up and she lost her grip, fell off, and he gave her a bit of a kicking in trying to get away. Not his fault — Jerry thinks it was a brown that struck at his hoof, and that would spook anyone. A brown snake — they're quite common round here, and poisonous, a bite can kill you in pretty short order. Anyway, Susie ended up with a badly broken leg, a cracked collarbone and quite a bit of bruising – she rolled herself into a ball which protected her from anything worse.

Jerry and the boys did what they could to make her comfortable, they always carry a first-aid kit along, and he got word back to us. We radio'd for the RFDS, and they were there pretty quick, flew her to the big hospital in Roma where they fixed her up. She's back home now, after a few days under obbo in case there were any complications, feeling sorry for herself and getting waited on hand and foot! She's allowed up now, hobbles around on a pair of crutches while we take the mickey out of her, but her Mum makes her rest most of the time. And this young lad has been riding all the way out from Mitchell on his motorbike every other day to see her! His name's Brett, and he's a really nice kid – he obviously thinks a lot of her, even if we didn't know of his existence before! He's a truckie, drives for the woodyard the other side of town, wants to get on the big rigs when he's older driving across the country.

All this has only reinforced Freddie's determination to be a Flying Doctor! He's working harder than ever at his lessons, doing real well — I think he might even make the grades he needs. I hope he does — it means so much to him. Anna's been fussing over Susie almost as much as Harrie — Alby's been pretending a kind of haughty indifference, but then he'll go and sit beside her for hours at a time, talking or even reading to her. Big softy underneath it all, my boy!

Sam and Ginny are settling in in their new house down in Alexandra Headland — it's a beautiful spot, we quite envy them! There's a lot of new development around there, and I think it's going to be one of the places to live, if you know what I mean? Land prices are rocketing there, they were lucky to buy when they did! We're off to spend Christmas with them in a few days, me and Harrie, Susie, Freddie and Anna. Alby's staying here with Jerry and the boys to look after the place — we usually have a kind of communal Christmas with them all, and I feel kind of guilty going off like this, but Jerry insisted we go and have a break and the other boys have all said the same. Maybe it sounds silly, but I think I'm going to miss them all! But it'll be great to have the holiday with my sis and her husband.

Your plans sound terrific, Steve — I'm so pleased that things are going so well for you all. Who knows, maybe one day we'll come back to the Old Country and take a holiday on one of your boats! The new boats you're having built sound ideal for the job, but I find it difficult to picture such a short narrowboat — I can't help imagining ones like our old boats. Send us a photo or two, okay? Have you still got the Rita? I know you're only using the Albert for the trips — what did you do with the butty?

Not much else to tell from down under! Harrie sends her love, as do the kids. And Sam and Ginny say Hi, and to remind you you owe them a letter!

All the best,

Mike

Midland Canal Holidays Ltd
Top Lock Wharf
Knowle
Warwickshire

Jan 7th 1970

Hi all!

Forgive the showing off - I couldn't resist using our new headed paper, just to show you how it looks. Not very fancy, but we wanted to make it look neat and modern - what do you think? We'll have the new phone lines in very soon, and the number added after the address.

How's Susie now? We were upset to hear about her accident, and everyone sends her their love and best wishes - tell her we're thinking of her, and hope she's very soon completely better. And who's this Brett lad - it sounds pretty serious if he's been going to so much trouble to come and see her!

Are you all back home now - how was Christmas? I hope you all had a great time - barbecue on the beach for Christmas dinner, was it? I can't imagine that, somehow! We had the usual good time - I still miss Mum's Christmas dinners, and I think everyone else does too, but Sylv and Ellie did it together this year, at our house, and it was marvelous to be all together. I think Dad loved it especially, surrounded by his grandchildren, spoiling them rotten!

He and I went to take a look at the first of our new boats the other day. They're looking really good - Chris Barney's designed a very good hull, based pretty much on the way our old boats were built, very nice long swims both ends so they should slip through the water nicely. There are some other people building new boats now, and some of the ones we've seen swim like a brick! They're too bluff all round, so the water can't get to the blades properly, and the fore-ends are much too square. But ours look really good - I can't wait to try one of them out!

They'll have a small saloon at the front, after a little open well-deck, and then the galley - behind that is the toilet and shower, and finally a cabin with three bunks in. In the saloon, there's a table and two padded benches which all rearranges into a double bed, so they can sleep five people altogether, the idea is that they'll be just right for a family with two or three kids, you see. We're thinking about maybe fitting the next ones out ourselves - after all, James and I have all the skills we need between us, and Dad's quite capable of doing a lot to help, and there's Billy too - but we'll have these ones done right out so that we can see how they go about it! And it means they will be ready in good time for Easter, when we want to have them available for hire. I'll take a few pictures and send them to you so you can see how they look! We'll have them painted in the same red and white, your old colours! They're going to be called the Knowle Star and the Knowle Gem - what do you think?

Bookings are coming in already for next season, mostly for the cruisers, but people are beginning to ask about the bigger boats when they know we're having them built. They'll have to be more expensive to hire, but that doesn't seem to be putting them off! And while it's quiet at this time of year, I'm expecting we'll get plenty of trips for the Albert once the spring arrives.

Yes, I've still got your old butty - you don't think I'd part with either of those boats, do you? The Rita doesn't get used at all, I'm afraid, so maybe it's a bit of a waste, but I couldn't sell her. I do look after her, we keep her pumped out and clean and smart, tied in the wide pound outside the house - and Dad, Billy and I have taken the pair out once or twice, just for the fun of doing it, and for old time's sake, I suppose. Back in the autumn, we ran them all the way down to Warwick and back - right down Hatton, just for fun! Would you believe it? It was a nice day, and it brought back so many memories - Dad said it would have been wonderful if you could have been with us, and he was right. Maybe one day?

Grace says to say thank you for the birthday card - we haven't let her open the parcel yet! It doesn't seem possible that she'll be a teenager just next week. Won't answer to Gracie any more! She's doing well in her new school, enjoying it even if she complains that the work is much harder. And Michael's doing well too at the little school in town. Ellie drops them both off, and picks them up after school, most days - but they both love it if Grandad does the school run, especially picking them up! They're really proud of him, that he used to run boats on the cut, and don't care a bit if he can't read and write! When he does pick them up, they're always late back because some of Grace's friends start chatting to him about the canal - and you know Dad! He can't resist talking to them, and Ellie's had to keep their meals warm more than once. What the other kids parents think I don't know - you'll remember how folk on the bank used to treat us! But it's all good for the future of the cut - one of her friends, she says, is trying to persuade his parents to hire a boat for their holiday.

Well, I seem to have gone on for ever about all our plans - how is life out there in the sun? Susie aside, we hope you're all well - give the kids our love, and to Sam and Ginny, and Carrie and Davey and the boys. Thanks for pictures - Ellie says you're still a handsome devil, Mikey, and Harrie is as pretty as ever. You both look so fit and well - the Australian life must suit you! And the kids all look amazing - it must be a really healthy lifestyle you all have. Tell

Susie we're all hoping she'll be up and about properly again very soon, and back on her horses!

That's all for now - take care, and write soon.

Steve.

January 26ᵗʰ 1970

Hi Steve, Ellie

Just a quick note to say thanks for the letter — it sounds like your plans are really coming together! Good for you — it's great to hear that everything's going well. And we're so pleased that your Dad seems to be enjoying life so much; we were worried about him when your Mum died, but it sounds as though he's still his old cheerful optimistic self. How old is he now? He must be well over seventy — give him our love, won't you?

And Harrie wanted to let you know that Susie is well on the way to recovery — thanks for your good wishes, she's promised to write herself but hasn't got around to it — you know what kids are like! She's still hobbling around the place with a crutch, because the doc insists she doesn't overstrain the leg yet, but other than that she's fine. She's been on a horse a few times lately, doesn't seem at all frightened by what happened, although Jerry won't let her go out with the boys yet — I think he's more upset about it than she is.

Like you, we had a great Christmas, with Sam and Ginny — she and Harrie looked after Christmas dinner, and we had a huge turkey and all the trimmings. Just like the old days when we all met up at your Mum's! Barbie on the beach for Boxing Day, cold turkey sandwiches and salad with burgers and snorkers on the grill. A traditional Aussie Christmas! We stayed over to New Year before going home — Alby and Jerry did a grand job of looking after things while we were away, not that I'd any doubts about them!

It's Australia Day today, so we're all having a day off apart from the odd chores that need doing every day. Alby's gone to have a few days with Sam and Ginny, and he rang last night to say they're going fishing out in the bay near a headland called Point Cartwright today, setting off at first light — keen beggars! But I quite envy them, to be honest — we went out in their boat a couple of times while we were down there, and it is a wonderful experience. They've got a nice boat, 20 feet with a light aluminium hull and a big outboard engine, goes a lot quicker than our old boats could have dreamed of! As it's Monday, we've had a long weekend in effect, and Josh and Laura have flown up to have a couple of days with Carrie. We shot into town for a few beers with them yesterday, had a good old catch-up yarn in the bar!

Young Brett seems like a nice kid — Susie tells us she'd met him in town a few times, and she seems to like him well enough. He's picked her up today on his motorbike, and they've gone in to join the other youngsters for a barbie at one of the parents houses in town. I don't know if it'll lead anywhere, but then she'll be eighteen in March — doesn't seem possible, does it? Freddie's out in the yard, playing with Anna — he's really good with his little sister, even if there is ten years between them!

Good for his bedside manner, I guess, if he does get to be a doc! I can see him going into children's medicine — he seems to get on well with the little ones, with Anna's friends when they come to call.

Not much else to tell — Harrie's sitting in the sun with a good book and a glass of cold beer, and I'm going to join her! Take care, and give our love to one and all,

Mike.

March 12th 1970

Hi Mike, Harrie

Sorry about the long silence, but I've been hanging on before writing because we were promised delivery of the Star - should have been here about ten days ago but there was a hold-up because they couldn't get the water heater. But it's here now - Billy and I brought it back from Braunston over the last two days.

It's a super little boat, Mike - handles really nicely, once you get used to it being only about two-thirds the length of a 'proper' boat! Swims very well, and the little two-cylinder engine is just right for it, plenty powerful enough with a bit in reserve, and with a nice big set of blades it even stops pretty well. And it looks a treat - Ellie's taken some pictures and I'll send you some once they're printed.

You'd be astonished at the inside, Mike - all mod cons, as they say! But that's what people are beginning to expect on their holidays now. It's got electric lights in the cabins, run off of the batteries, and it uses bottles of gas to run the cooker and the water heater - yes, there's even running water, hot and cold! There's a tank in the fore-end, below the well-deck, and an electric pump which supplies taps in the galley and toilet, and even a shower! It's a bit cramped, but it works pretty well - I tried it out on the way back. The Gem is almost ready, too - I'm going to send Dad and young Bill to fetch that one - but they don't know that yet! I reckon they'll have a grand time bringing it back, Dad thinks the world of his grandson and Bill thinks his granddad is the greatest, they get on so well together.

Bookings are looking very good this year too - most of the cruisers are out over the Easter holiday, and then right on into the summer, and the Star's got its first hires then too. The first family using it are friends of Grace's - a lad she knows from school and his parents and younger brother. I've let them have it at half price, and they're going to give me a report on what they think of it, any problems they have and so on.

How are things with you all? I imagine Susie must be about fully recovered by now - give her our love, and wish her a happy birthday. Card and present are on their way! I bet Alby enjoyed his break on the coast - it sounds great, going out on the ocean for a day's lazy fishing when the sun's shining! Quite a contrast with us at the moment - it's just about above freezing outside, we're having a bit of a cold snap but they're saying it'll warm up again in a day or two. Warm will mean maybe 45 degrees, if we're lucky - what have you got, about 90? Lucky beggars!

Say Hi to all the kids for us, and to Sam and Ginny too of course - how are they getting on, how's Sam's new job going? Wish them all the best from us.

Keep in touch - Ellie says she'll write with some pictures of the boat in a week or two.

Cheers
Steve.

March 23rd 1970

Hello Mikey and Harrie!

Just a quickie to send you the pictures of our new boats. Stevie insisted I got them off to you straight away – he's so proud of them, he's like a dog with two tails, fussing around with a big grin on his face. I think they look really good, very smart in your old colours with the signwriting on them; we all hope they'll be popular enough to pay for themselves, although we have to charge more for their hire than the old cruisers.

Things are looking good so far – the cruisers are pretty well booked up for the early part of the summer, and the new boats are slowly picking up bookings too. The Star is out right now, with the family of one of Grace's schoolfriends on board – we've not heard anything, so they are presumably managing all right! Billy is getting the Gem ready as I write, it's going out for the first time at the weekend. Do write and tell us what you think of them – your opinion means a lot to Stevie, Mike.
He's already talking about buying more of the same type of boat next year, probably selling off some of the cruisers to help pay for them. I think he's getting a bit ahead of himself, that we ought to wait and see just how well they do this year, but you know my

Steve! His Dad is just as enthusiastic, and I have to tell him off for egging him on from time to time!

Bill really runs the Albert now, as his own part of the business, and now that their bookings are picking up with the spring coming on, young Bill's spending most of his time acting as his crew. The two of them get on so well together, and young Bill is as good as anyone at handling that big boat – they take turn and turn about steering and talking to the passengers, but if we get a school trip Steve's Dad does the talking! The teachers and kids all love him, because he can tell them what it used to be like working on the boats. Young Bill is supposed to be going on to college after his year out, but I'm not sure he will – I think if there is room for him he'll want to stay here and work for the business, with his Dad and Uncle! And Grandad, of course!

Emily's home for Easter – with a young man in tow! He's a fellow she met at Uni, seems like a nice kid, studying architectural design. Billy's a bit wary of him – no-one's good enough for his little girl, as you can imagine! But this lad, Danny Norris, is trying really hard to get on with him, and I think he's winning him over. He and Emily seem really stuck on each other – but I guess we'll have to wait and see where it all goes in the end.

Violet is studying for her O levels this year, working hard, bless her! She wants to do well and go on to A levels so that she can be a PE teacher – still swimming, and training hard too, because she's been picked to swim for the county at a big tournament in a week or two. Linda's in 'big school' now, at the same school as our Grace but a year behind her of course – they get on fine at home, but ignore each other at school! Typical kids.

Grace is doing very well now, after a bit of a slow start – she found the work at senior school hard going for a while, but now she's really buckled down to it. And Michael's doing well too, his teacher says he's a good kid, helpful and co-operative in class – not like the little tearaway we get when he's at home! He has a knack of getting in the way, under your feet all the time – Billy's always having to chase him away when he's trying to work on one of the boats. The boy doesn't mean any harm, he's just so curious about everything, and Billy loves him really – but he always seems to ask a question just at the wrong moment and distract him!

I think that's about all of our news. Everyone sends their love and best wishes, and Michael keeps asking when he can go and visit his Uncle Mike and Auntie Harriet. If he gets under our feet much more, you might find a large wriggly package delivered to your door one of these days!

Take care, and write soon,

Love, Ellie.

April 14th 1970

Hi Steve, Ellie

Thanks for your letters, and the pictures of the new boats. They do look really great, Steve, and the cabins — talk about the lap of luxury! When you think about the way we used to live in the boats, with just the old back cabin, a toilet in the engine-hole and fresh water in the cans, you wonder how we ever managed. And what about your Mum, bringing up a bunch of kids in those conditions? We never thought twice about it, did we — it was just how life was, but when you look back now and compare it with these new holiday boats of yours! You could live in one of them very comfortably indeed — but there'd be nowhere to put the load, would there!

How are the bookings going? I do hope they prove to be popular, it must have been quite a big investment for you, but from what you said it sounds as though it will pay off. I suppose, when you think about it, I can see why people might want to go boating for a holiday — I mean, we always enjoyed the trips, didn't we? It was just the hard work, loading and unloading, and the pressure to get there and get paid — if you could just cruise along, especially in the better weather, and enjoy the scenery and the actual boating without any pressure it would be very pleasant. And when you look at all the comforts of home in these boats, too, you can see why they might be an alternative to a week by the seaside! Anyway, we are all rooting for you, hoping you have a decent summer and a good season.

Thanks for the family update, Ellie! It's good to know everyone's okay — my namesake sounds like quite a character! If he gets to be too much, pack him up and send him out, we'll teach him to ride horses and round up cattle! Seriously, it would be wonderful to see him sometime — if you could ever spare the time and the money, come and see us. Our summer is your winter, remember, so it would be when your boats are not being used — think about it? We'd all love to see you again, and we could put you up here — might be a bit of a squeeze if you all came, but we'd manage!

There's not much to tell from this end, life goes on much as ever. Susie and Brett is looking more and more serious as time goes by, he's a really nice lad but he seems a bit wary, somehow — I wonder if he's just nervous about going out with the daughter of a landowner! His family are what we might call working-class — it doesn't matter to us, we think of ourselves the same way! But they only know us as the owners of Marloo Creek, and it's a pretty big spread. I've told him all about where we came from, from the boats and so on, but he still seems kind of nervous around Harrie and me.

The other kids are all doing fine. Alby's really in the swing of running this place now, working with Jerry — makes my life very easy! But Jerry did say the other day that he's getting a bit too old for it. He still won't admit just how old he is, but Harrie and I worked out from odd things he's said that he must be nearer seventy than sixty. His parents came here from Ireland just after the First World War, and he's admitted to being a teenager then! I've told him, on the quiet, that if he wants to retire he'll have a home here with us for as long as he wants it — he's become very much a part of the family, and the kids all think the world of him. That said, I can't see him giving it away for a while yet!

Sam's getting on very well — and thoroughly enjoying life on the coast. The boatyard there is keeping him busy, and Ginny says he's beginning to get a reputation for having a knack with the big outboard motors they use on most of the boats down there. And he's been earning a bit on the side piloting 'trips around the bay'! Not so far from what you're doing with the Albert! Ginny's fine — they're getting used to the idea of not having kids of their own, but she said to me on the phone the other day that they might think about adopting, once life is really settled for them.

Carrie and Davey were here yesterday, with the two boys — they're all fine, enjoying life at the pub, building the business up a bit it seems. They do rooms, and there's been a growing interest in city folk coming out to take a gander at the outback — now the worst of the rains are over, they're hoping for a few more visitors. The road the other side of town was washed out for a while, but the river's gone down again now. Kyle's a nice kid, eight now, blue eyes and freckles like his Dad and a thatch of blond hair — dead keen on sports! He had all of ours and his brother, and Brett as well, out in the yard playing cricket most of the afternoon. Todd's darker, like Carrie, quieter — I think he's got the brains of the family! He'll be seven this winter, in August, he was telling me — dropping hints, I suspect! Harrie took some pictures of them all, we'll send you some when they come back from the shop.

Anyhow, I guess that's all for now. Take care of yourselves, pass our love all around;

Mike and Harrie.

Interlude

1970

November 14th 1970

Dear Mike, Harrie and the kids,
Here we are again, Christmas on the way! Ellie's packing a parcel for you, and I wanted to write to bring you up to date with our news so I'll put this letter in with the presents!

Sorry I haven't written before - we've had such a busy time of it! Ellie's dropped you the odd letter, I know, so you'll know we've been doing well this summer - the new narrowboats have proved to be very popular. People like the better facilities they offer, and the fact there's more room in them - both of them have been out almost constantly since Easter! One is even booked for two weeks over Christmas - we've told the people that they're taking a chance with the weather, but they seem happy to risk it.

And the Albert has had a busy year too - word has really got around now, and we get more groups from word of mouth than we do from any advertising! Some of them like to have food on board, if they're having a longer trip, so Ellie and Sylvie do a cold buffet between them - the customers seem to like it, and it adds to the income because we can charge a very reasonable extra for it and still show a profit!

I'm going to have two more steel-hull narrowboats built this year - they're already on order, we should have the first one at the beginning of January - and Billy, Dad and I are going to fit them out ourselves. With James's help and advice, of course!

So we're doing just great, Mike - but the sad news is that the old boats are finished. We heard a while ago that the jam 'ole was finishing - and that was the last contract working on the cut. It was supposed to end in August, apparently, but they had a last load delivered a few weeks ago - and that was it. No more long-distance boats working anywhere. We hadn't seen any this way for quite a while, so I guess we knew, but to know for sure it's all over is just so sad. Our whole way of life, Mike, gone for good.

There are still some short-haul jobs running - around Birnigum, they're still using some of the Joeys for local coal deliveries and things like that, and the rubbish boats to Salvage Turn, and someone said the lime-juice run from Brentford to Boxmoor's still going, but the idea that no more boats are running down the Junction is difficult to believe.

The cut will go on, though. We've proved that, I think - holiday boats, leisure, that's where it'll be for the future. Much of the system is in a pretty bad state, and there's a constant war going on between British Waterways Board who run it all now and pressure groups like the Inland Waterways Association to get things improved. We joined the IWA as a 'corporate member' a few years ago - they seem to be doing a good job for the waterways, on the whole.

Did I ever tell you that part of the Stratford Cut is open again? A local group had been working on it for years, and they re-opened the length from Lapworth down to Stratford back in 1964. They're working on the rest of it now, and hoping to have it open right up to the Worcester cut in the next few years. That'll be good for us - it'll open up another route for our customers. We've had one or two do the run down to Stratford in recent years, and the Star went down there at least three times this summer! The stretch up Lapworth to Kings Norton will make a round trip for people, round through Birnigum and back down through the old thirteen, Ashted Six and Camp Hill. Or even Aston and the Garrison, if they're really keen! Some of our hirers actually _like_ routes with lots of locks - no accounting for some people, is there?

Ellie is going to write with all the family news, so I won't go into that! Have a great Christmas, everyone.

All our best wishes

Steve

November 15th 1970

Hello Mike, Harriet and all!

Just a quick note to wish you all a very merry Christmas – hope you like the presents! Grey, cold and miserable here at the moment – think of us while you're enjoying the sunshine! Are you home this year? What about Sam and Ginny – are they still all right and enjoying life?

All the family here are fine – Steve and Billy have been working very hard this year, with eight small boats and the two narrowboats to look after – they've all been out most of the summer, so it's kept us all on our toes! And Bill's doing fine – he had a bout of shingles a while ago, I think I told you at the time, but he's got completely over it now. The doctor says that he's in amazing shape for a man of his age – he's actually admitted to being about 75! Young Bill's gone off to college – he was in two minds about it, but in the end he took his Dad's advice. Even if he wants to come back here and work for the firm, a degree in Chemistry isn't going to do him any harm in the future, and he can see the sense of that for himself.

Violet passed her O levels – I think you knew? She's still at school, doing biology, maths and PE for A level. Still wants to teach PE; and she is a fixture in the County swimming team now!

Emily will be home from Uni soon — she's still going out with her Danny, and I can see that leading to wedding bells in time! Linda's very well too — getting over a bout of 'flu, there's a lot of it about this year, but she's well on the mend and doing well in school.

Gracie will be a teenager in January — it doesn't seem possible, does it? And I mustn't call her that any more! My name is Grace, Mother — I can hear her telling me off now! Michael is the same as ever, hurtling around the place and getting under everyone's feet but getting glowing reports from his teachers — how can one kid look so different to different people? But we all love him of course — and he's always a favourite with our customers when they come to collect or return the boats, often 'helps' his Dad or Billy with the hand-overs and instruction time.

Do you get the English television programmes out there in Australia? I think a lot of them get sold abroad after they've been shown here. I quite like what they're calling 'soap operas' — when I have the time to watch them! Stevie can't bear them - but we all had to watch one called Coronation Street last week because Gabriel had a part in it, playing a gypsy who's passing through and causing trouble. With his dark eyes and hair he really looks the part, you can imagine! He's going to be in for the next few weeks as well, but it's only a short-term part. He's doing so well – and still such a nice boy, not at all big-headed about his success. He's doing an engineering degree with the Open University in his spare time, making sure he's got something to fall back on, as he puts it! I expect you'll have heard from Joe and Grace anyway?

I think that's all of our news – do drop us a line back with your latest. Have a wonderful Christmas!

All our love,

Ellie.

December 4th 1970

Hi Steve, Ellie, etc!

Thank you for the presents, and your letters. We've managed to stop Anna from opening hers, so far at least, told her Father Christmas won't bring her anything else if she does! I'm not sure she's convinced – after all, she's six now, and beginning to question her old Dad's logic at times!

It sounds as though everything is going well for you all back there in the Old Country – we're delighted for you! We've heard from Joe, and written back – it's good to know that Jack is doing well, and Rosie a Mum, too? How about that! We do get Corrie here, some time after it's shown in the UK – can't be doing with such things myself, but Harrie watches sometimes – now we have mains electric laid on, we don't have to be so stingy with the power at home any more, and it helps around the property as well. We'll look out for that storyline when it gets to us!

You're right, it's so sad to know the boats are all finished. I suppose we saw it coming, even before we left – perhaps it's surprising that they kept on as long as this, especially after the big freeze you had, seven years ago now? Harrie and I were really rather upset at your news, even if we both knew it had to happen one day. It set us reminiscing, last night, talking about the old days and the people we knew – it's difficult to imagine a world with no boats plying the canals any more. Harrie got a bit weepy, and I must admit I felt like joining her! All the good days we had, and the evenings with other boaters in the Boat at Stoke Bruin or the Red Lion, the Spotted Cow at Buckby or the Five Bells in Brentford – to think that none of that can ever happen again? But life goes on, my friend, come what may.

Everyone here is well – Alby's very much my right-hand man now, and I'm so proud of him. Jerry is gradually handing more and more responsibility over to him, beginning to take a back seat, but I can't see him ever 'retiring'! He's one of those guys who'll keep going til he drops, but I've told him to take some time out whenever he wants to, to go and stay with his sister for a break — not that he's taking me up on it as yet! Freddie's doing fine, still studying hard but passing his grades along the way — how can he possibly be sixteen? He's a great kid, tries very hard to be a grumpy teenager, especially with me, but doesn't quite pull it off somehow.

And Susie — have I got a yarn for you there! You remember I said how young Brett always seemed kind of shy around Harrie and me? Well, now we know why! He's real good kid, a year older than her, and well thought of around the town and by the boss of the woodyard — he drives trucks for them, goes delivering as far out as Roma and into the outback stations and sometimes has one of the big rigs they use to haul in the felled trees. And it seems he's pretty stuck on our girl, too. He came to see me a while back, wanted to talk in private — what he wanted to tell me is that he's part aborigine. His grandfather was a pure-blood blackfella. Brett's kind of dark, I guess, with deep brown eyes, so you can see it if you know — not that we'd ever thought about it. And as I told him, it makes no difference to us at all! There's still a lot of prejudice here towards the Abos, a lot of the whites look down on them and the authorities even snatch half-caste kids and put them in institutions if they can find them — for no good reason, as far as I can see. Doesn't seem credible, does it? Anyway, he was worried that we'd turn against him when we found out, but I've put him right on that score! We had a good old yarn afterwards, and he's much more relaxed around here since. Harrie thinks the world of him, so I think we might end up with a truckie son-in-law some time soon — I'll keep you posted!

I reckon our Anna would get on with my namesake like a house on fire, from what you say about him! She's a real outback tomboy, always on the move, never stops — can get pretty tiring sometimes just keeping up with her, but we wouldn't change her for the world.

Sam and Ginny are coming here for the holiday — we went to them last year — and Carrie and Davey and the boys are coming for the day too. It'll be great to be all together again! Harrie is going to roast a turkey the day before, so we'll be tucking in to cold turkey and stuffing and salad for Christmas dinner, probably out in the backyard with plenty of cold beers. Then no doubt the kids will have a game of cricket, and I expect we'll all end up in the creek at some point to keep cool... Then New Year — Josh and Laura are coming to stay with Carrie, so that'll mean another barbie!

Have a great Christmas and New Year, take care of yourselves,

With our love,

Mike.

Part Four

1979

July 14th 1979

Hello Mikey, Harriet and all!

How are you all? Well, we hope, and enjoying life! How's it feel to hit the big 5-0, Mike? Your party sounds like it was a really grand affair – are you doing the same for Harrie in September?

Sorry I haven't written for a while – we're so busy here! If you'd told us, fifteen years ago, just how popular this business would be we would never have believed you. I'll lean on Stevie to drop you a line himself – it's still his baby, and I know he'll want to tell you more himself. But you know him – getting him to put pen to paper these days is a job in itself!

The kids are all well, and send their love: Grace is still talking about the great time she had with you in Aus last winter, and about having Christmas dinner on the beach with Sam and Ginny! Steve is getting more and more impatient with Michael, I'm afraid – the boy leaves school this month, and he still can't make up his mind what he wants to do! Kids! He and his Dad have spent hours talking about ideas and possibilities – Steve would like him to join the business in some ways, but he realizes that it's not what Mike wants to do – but the blessed kid won't settle on anything else either! He still goes on about going to see you one day, and we've promised him he can — perhaps now would be a good time? It might give him time to think about his future — how about it, would you be prepared to put up with a cranky teenager for a few weeks?

Billy and Sylvie are fine, and their kids are all okay too. Emmie's looking much better now, after the hard time she had with little Connor — the doctors have told her she shouldn't have any more children. I think she and Danny are disappointed, but they've got two lovely kids in him and Chelsea already, so it could be worse! Danny's been promoted to assistant curator at the museum now, so they're a bit better off too. We don't hear from young Bill very often — he's quite settled down in Bristol with his Alison, and doing well for himself, as far as we can gather! Vi is really enjoying her new job at Northampton School — coming to the end of her first year there, and so pleased she decided to take it after all. She's sharing a flat with another of the teachers, and having a great time by the sound of it! Linda's off to college in Coventry this year — I think she's been influenced by Vi's success, talking about becoming a maths teacher later. We'll see!

Last we heard from Joe, they were all okay — have you heard from them lately? We saw Gabriel in his new film the other day — it still seems incredible that such a big star is our nephew! We're all so proud of him — but on the odd times we see him, he's still the same lovely, dozy kid we always knew! Joe had to retire from the truck-driving because of his back – I think it runs in the family, remember how bad his Dad was as he got older? And I doubt if all the years of hard shovelling on the boats did him any good, either. He's got a part-time job delivering cars now – keeps him happy and out from under Gracie's feet! And it's much easier on his back than the big trucks.

Steve's Dad goes on the same as ever! He just doesn't change – I swear he looks just the same as he did twenty years ago. A bit greyer, maybe, but he's as fit as ever – still loves running the Albert, and talking to the passengers. We get a lot of school parties now, and the kids all think the world of him when he gets to telling them about the old days, on the horse-boat with his parents before the First World War – I sometimes wonder if they really believe that he's that old! He must be about 85 now, we reckon.

Anyway, I think that's all of our news for now. Do write back, let us know how you're all doing – how's Alby's girl taking to life in the bush after the big city? And did Freddie qualify from medical college – or is that next year? I lose track of the years, I'm afraid.

Take care of yourselves,

With all our love,

Ellie

August 2nd 1979

Dear Ellie & Steve,

    Thanks for the letter — good to know everyone's doing okay back there in the UK. Has Gracie got herself a fella now? Last we heard she had this lad Alan hanging around — is that still on? I know she loved it out here, and it was great to celebrate her birthday with her; we almost had to push her on board the plane to go home! Give her our love, tell her we'd love to see her again if she wants to fly out here any time.

    About Michael — of course, if he'd like to come and see us we'd be only too happy to have him stay here for a while. We've talked about him coming over here before, and like you say now might be a good time if he's still undecided what the future holds for him. Just let us know when he's going to turn up! I guess Sam and Ginny could meet him from Brisbane airport and either run him out here or throw him on a flight to Mitchell or Roma.

Our tribe are pretty much the same as ever. Brett and Susie have moved to Longreach with the grandkids – it's easier for them there now that Brett's in his new job – did we tell you? He's driving for an outfit called Thompson Trucking, known as the 'Double T', gets to go all over Queensland and across the Territory, right up around the Top End to Darwin is one of his regular trips. Vanessa's growing up, five next November – she's a pretty little thing, all big brown eyes and the cutest smile. Takes after her dad, luckily! And Adam will be two after Christmas. I still find it hard to believe I'm a granddad, you know? They're going to be here for Harrie's birthday, of course. Freddie's coming back from College for the do as well – Harrie insists she doesn't want a big do at the pub, so we're going to have hers here at the house. We'll lay on a big barbie, some kind of music, and plenty of beer of course! Everyone's coming – Sam and Ginny and the girls, Carrie and Davey and Todd (Kyle will be away in the Air

Force by then). Josh is hoping to make it, but with Laura pregnant again it might be difficult for them. It would be great if Michael was here by then — we're planning for the last weekend in September, but don't ask me what the dates are! We could show him a proper Aussie wing-ding — it's his birthday too, isn't it? What'll he be, seventeen this year?

Lesley's settling in just fine, bless her! You know how long it's taken Alby to persuade her to give up her career in Toowoomba to come here and join him — I guess it shows how much she loves our boy that she's finally done it. He's just as stuck on her — she doesn't know it, but he'd been trying to find out if he could get a decent job there if she'd decided she couldn't give up the bright lights. But now she's here, she seems to be loving the life — I've offered her the job of company accountant, after all it would be a shame to waste her talents.

I'm relieved, as you can imagine — what we'd have done without Alby I don't know! He's pretty much in charge here now, alongside me. Jerry's just about retired – well, as retired as he'll ever be, I guess! He still goes out around the property with the boys quite a bit, and gets stuck in with them, but he knows it's at his own choice now. He lives in the old slab hut, and seems to love it – I guess it's like the old days when he first came out to Marloo Creek.

Alby and Les have the spare house, the one we built for Sam and Ginny when we first came here, and they seem quite settled and happy. Harrie keeps dropping hints about more grandchildren, but they both quietly ignore her – all in good time, I guess – but it would be good to see the Baker name going on into the next generation! Maybe Freddie will find a decent girl in time – right now he's so committed to his studies that he just doesn't have that much time for socializing. It's his 25th in September too, so the party'll be a pretty big do all round! He qualifies at the end of this year, in November – our academic year's six months out of kilter with yours too, just like the seasons — our kids have their long holiday in December and January, over Christmas. He says he's got a girl in college, but we don't think it's really that serious.

You should see Sam and Ginny's girls now — I'll get Harrie to take some snaps of them next time we see them and send them to you. We went over there for Kalina's birthday last month — she's nine now, and the most gorgeous little girl you can imagine! She's got her natural father's black hair and big dark eyes, but her features are more Caucasian; the best of both worlds, you might say, an incredibly pretty kid. Little Brooke's a cutie too — she's not so dark, got more of her mother's colouring. She was seven back in the autumn, in March.

Harrie and I are so pleased that they decided to adopt in the end — Ginny's such natural mother it would have been a shame for her not to have kids to bring up even if they aren't really her own. And their choice to adopt half-caste kids caused a bit of a stir, if you remember? It wasn't that long after the authorities had given up the idea of forcibly 'emancipating' mixed-birth kids and sticking them in asylums — but attitudes here in Australia have changed a lot in the last few years, thank goodness!

Carrie and Davey are doing well with the pub — Josie's still about, but she doesn't get involved these days, leaves it all to the kids. Kyle's been accepted for training in the RAAF, goes off for his induction next week; and Todd wants to be a brickie. He's sixteen this month, and he's got an apprenticeship with a building firm based in Roma, starts in October. Things are different here — a fully-passed brickie, or any kind of tradesman for that matter, is looked on almost as a professional man. Not like back home, where they'd be 'just workmen'! And Queensland has the fastest growing population in Australia, so the demand for qualified men in the building trade is huge — they get damned good money, too!

Not much else to tell from down under — do get Steve to drop me a line, it would be good to have the latest news of the cut, and an up-date on the state of the business! How many boats have you got now? Come on Stevie, get the pen out!

Give our love to one and all, and do parcel Michael up and send him out to us if you can't think of anything else to do with him!

All our love,

Mike.

August 22nd 1979

Hi Mikey!

 Sorry - I've been meaning to write to you for ages, and Ellie keeps badgering me about it, but it's just been so busy here, I haven't got round to it. Why did I ever go into the hire-boat business? I never get a moment's peace nowadays!

 Ellie and I were talking about it the other night, and something she said was quite right - if you'd told us, back when Dad and I first set the Albert up as a tripper, and bought the first of those little cabin cruisers, just how big the business would get, we'd never have believed you! It was almost a matter of desperation - do you remember? The trade had about finished, and it was just a way of keeping the Albert working, and making a few bob to keep the bread on the table! Now look at us - nearly twenty boats, all of them new-built steel narrowboats, and more customers than we know what to do with! The number of people we have to turn down, especially in the spring, is amazing. Bad, really - they have to go somewhere else, and so we might lose them for all time.   But we have a good relationship with an outfit called Wyvern Shipping - they're down the Junction at Linslade, and we usually suggest them if we can't accommodate someone.   The people there do the same for us, so it helps everyone. The folks who run it, the Griffins, came from the carrying trade like us, not Johnny-come-latelys like some of the other hire bases.

As you'll have gathered, our bank manager now thinks the sun shines out of our account!   He's been great, over the years - lent us the money to buy the Gem and the Star to begin with, and hasn't hesitated to support us the same way ever since.   I try to manage without borrowing as much as I can, but it does help with buying the new boats every winter when we don't have the income we do in the summer.   I've got two more on order now for next year, which will take us to 21 boats - I suppose you could say we've come of age! They're being built at Market Harborough, in the old basin there - steel hulls, composition tops, with Lister air-cooled engines.   We're doing the fit-outs here as usual - Billy's become a really good carpenter and joiner over the years, and we get very good reports of our boats in the Waterways World - that's a glossy magazine all about the canals. I'll send you a few copies sometime!

Both the new boats will be 65-footers. We had that one built a while ago, and it's been very popular - it sleeps up to ten, and we get groups like scouts and sports teams hiring it as well as bigger families. Even had a hen party on it for a week last June! I don't think they got very far, to judge from the number of empty wine bottles we took off it later! We did have to throw one stag party off the boat last year - they got a bit too carried away on the lager and caused trouble down in Warwick. Two of them ended up in the cells overnight, so we went and brought the boat back. It's handy having a couple of old boaters around - I mean, you wouldn't argue with Billy when he's roused, would you, even if he is over fifty! We called that one the Ark Royal, when someone said it looked like an aircraft carrier, so the next two will be the Eagle and the Illustrious!

This is still very much a family business, despite its growth, as you'll know

- we do employ people, a full-time mechanic to help Billy and some girls who help out part-time with the cleaning on the weekends when we turn the boats around. Ellie and Sylvie run that part of it - I'm proud of the way they always turn them out spick and span, and it helps to bring the customers back, sometimes year after year! Grace's working in the office now, doing most of the bookings and answering the phones - having a pretty face to greet people when they come doesn't hurt either! And the Albert's very much Dad's baby now - someone has to crew with him, of course. One of us does it in the week, usually, but there's a young kid from the town who helps him at the weekend - Martin started cycling over a couple of years ago, after he'd come on a school trip, just for the fun of it, but now he's a great help. He's only just fourteen, but he's good with the passengers, polite and helpful, and he's a nice-looking boy. And Dad's taught him to steer the boat - he's very good, too. I pay him for what he does, and he says it's better than having a paper-round!

And Michael - I don't know what we're going to do with him! He's my son, and I love him dearly, but I wish he'd make up his mind what he wants to do with his life. He's not stupid, far from it, done well in school, but he just seems to have no direction if you know what I mean. Ellie said you'd offered to have him out with you for a while - perhaps that would be a good thing. He's always said, since he was little, that he wanted to go and see his Uncle Mike, and maybe now's the right time. Perhaps you can drum some sense into him! Anyway, we've looked into it and booked a flight at the end of the month for him. He arrives at Brisbane airport at 11.35 on Sept 2nd - in the morning, you'll be pleased to know! I hope that's okay with you all? He's over the moon about it, can't stop talking about seeing you all! You can keep him as long as you like - I expect he'll love having his birthday out there with you, and being part of Harrie's party.

We've got him a new camera for his birthday, and we'll give it to him before he leaves. Make him work for his living while he's there, it'll do him good!

Anyway Mike, I guess that's about all I have to tell you. Drop us a line, let us know that Michael gets there in one piece! And give our love to all the family;

Steve.

September 7th 1979

Hello Steve, Ellie;

You'll be pleased to know that Michael got here safely. Sam and Ginny met him at the airport on Sunday, and he stayed overnight with them, then they all drove out here the next day and stayed over until yesterday. Bit of a crowd, but we squeezed them all in somehow! They'd got permission for the girls to be out of school for a few days to meet their pommie cousin, and we had a great time with everyone together here — Carrie and Davey had a day with us too, and Todd and Mike got on together like a house on fire! Mike's going to spend the weekend with them in Mitchell, Harrie's going to drop him over there later in the Chrysler.

One question, Stevie — how the Hell did an ugly bugger like you ever produce such a handsome kid? He's got to take after Ellie's family! He's such a nice kid too — so polite and well-behaved. To be frank, we were kind of expecting a difficult, grumpy teenager, but in fact he's a great kid — everyone's taken a liking to him already. We had a great laugh at his expense the other day — Alby put him on the back of a horse, and we lost count of the times he fell off again! Didn't do himself any real damage, just a bruise or two, and he was laughing as hard as the rest of us. He got the drop of it in the end — Anna's planning to take him out riding around the property next week.

Looks like the party's going to be a great occasion — there're so many birthdays this month! Harrie's 50th, of course, and Freddie's 25th — Anna was fifteen on Wednesday, and it turns out that Mike'll be seventeen on the Saturday of the barbie! I reckon we're all going to need a week to get over it! Carrie's laying in an extra order of VB for us, in time for the do — that's my usual tipple out here. It's a rather darker beer than the usual Fosters or Carlton, a bit more like we were used to back home, brewed down in Victoria — VB stands for Victoria Bitter. Maybe I shouldn't tell you, but Mike quite enjoyed the stubbie I gave him the other night when we were all sitting around yarning on the veranda. Things tend to be a bit more easy-going out here — even Anna'll enjoy the odd cold beer on a hot day! Don't worry, we won't turn your boy into an alcy!

Anyway, got to go now as Harrie's banging the gong for lunch. Great to hear that things are going so well for you all in the UK — I'll write again soon, let you know if Michael survives life down under!

All the best,

Mikey.

September 23rd 1979

Hi Mikey, Harriet –

Glad to hear our lad got there all right – aren't you all fed up with him by now? I suppose we'd perhaps given you the wrong idea of him – he's not a bad kid, it's just that lack of knowing what he wants to do that gets me frustrated with him. He's not stupid, either – he got eight O levels, did he tell you? Good ones, too. And you're right, he takes after his Mum's side of the family! I gather he looks a lot like James, his granddad, did at his age, tall and broad-shouldered, with that wavy hair – not that his granddad's got much of his left now!

I hope he's enjoying himself? Have you got him working, or is he just lazing around in the sun? Tell him we miss him, and his Mum's worrying about him on horseback – do they do seatbelts for horses? And if he gets a taste for beer he'll have to buy his own when he gets back here!

Things here are much the same as ever – we had the first of the new boats delivered this week, and Billy's started on fitting it out. The cut itself is getting

209

better, on the whole - BW have at last been spending some money, serious money, on dredging and maintenance over the last few years, so it's easier to get around in a lot of places. But you'll never guess what they've done now! They've closed Blisworth Tunnel - of all the idiotic ideas! Their excuse is that the ground in the middle of the hill's been shifting, making it unsafe - but it hasn't fallen in in what, a hundred and seventy years? I suppose if what they say is right, it'll need to be sorted out - but was it really necessary to close it altogether? And how long is it going to take? They say they haven't got the money to do it, even, so I think we're looking at a long stoppage, years even. If they eventually do it - there's been talk of just leaving it closed! They're saying you can use the Oxford cut to get to London and back - I suppose you can - but who would want to? And what about all the people who like to go round in circles - even from here, we've had hirers go all the way around, down the Junction, up the Thames and back up the Oxford. You can't do that now. Oh well, I suppose we'll just have to wait and see - but all the hire companies are lobbying to get it done quickly, and the IWA are on side too.

It's not all bad though - did I ever tell you that they did eventually get the Stratford cut open again? It was about five years ago now - good for us, because it opened up the old top road route into Birmingham, up Lapworth and onto the Worcester cut. Gives our hirers another option!

And you won't believe the laugh we had a couple of weeks ago. A call came in from a guy who'd hired the Emerald, and Grace couldn't make head nor tail of what he was trying to tell her. Billy went out to them to see what was wrong - and when he came back, he couldn't tell us for laughing! They'd got something around the blades, and followed instructions as far as getting the weed hatch open - we have a kind of hatch made in the counter, so you can get to the propeller to clear rubbish off it if you need to, much easier that they way we used to have to drag it off with a shaft from outside! Anyway, this guy'd got the lid off - and then set about trying to bail out the water so that he could reach the prop! What some of them use for common sense I'll never know - Billy reckons he kept a straight face while he put the fellow right, but I'm not sure I believe him!

We've had a few laughs over the years - I've told you about some of them, I know. I've still never worked out how that fellow got the Diamond so well stemmed up that we had to get a crane to it - he must have been going Hell for leather when he hit those collapsed copings! I told you, if you remember? The fore-end was all of a foot out of the water - and all because his hat blew off!

It's Sunday afternoon here - a nice day, quite warm and the sun's out. Dad's happy - he's got a local W.I. on the Albert today, and I expect he's having a grand time chatting up all the old ladies! He said he'd let young Martin steer today, if he wanted to - and knowing that lad he won't have taken any persuading. They'll be back soon, so I'd better go down to meet them.

Say hi to everyone for us, and tell that boy of mine he doesn't need to hurry back, we're managing okay without him - not that I harbor any illusions that he might think otherwise! Seriously, give him our love, but tell him he can stay as long as he wants, and as long as you're prepared to put up with him! Once he's got an idea of what he wants to do, let me know - if we need to look for college courses for him, we'll try and get something organized for next year. So you can keep him until then - please? We do miss him, of course, in all honesty - but don't tell him that!

Bye for now,

Steve.

October 7th 1979

Hi Steve, Ellie.

Thanks for your letter Steve — you talking about the laughs you've had set me and Harrie yarning the other night, talking about the old days on the boats. We were all lounging under the veranda after a hard day, with Alby and Les and the kids — Anna and Michael, and Freddie was still here after the party. I told them all the tale about how I wound up on the boats — my kids had heard it before, but I don't think Mike had? He was fascinated! It's so long ago now — but still perhaps the best days of my life. I don't think about it much now, but talking brought it all back.

And we talked about some of the things that happened — you remember how we lost the old Sycamore? The kids didn't believe us at first, that we'd run up on a safe around Olton! Dad never did like that Northwich boat we got in its place, bless him. I wonder what he'd have made of where we are now? And Mike had a good laugh when I told him about the time you nearly turned a lock around in front of me, do you remember? You looked so embarrassed! Too busy thinking about Ellie to be looking what you were doing! That must have been about the last trip you made on the boats, wasn't it? Next time we saw you, you were all on the bank at Knowle, if I remember right.

The party was a great success, everyone had a grand time. We had bodies everywhere, that night! Most of our friends from the town had come over, as well as all the family, and a lot of beer vanished in a few hours – there were people sleeping in all sorts of places when I got up the next morning. I'm afraid Michael had a bit more than was good for him – he was wandering around looking very sorry for himself all that day. Still, he's learnt his lesson! He's out with Anna today, they're riding out around the place – they seem to get on very well together. She's still a real Aussie tomboy, loves riding and helping around the animals, even goes out with the boys working around the property — when her Mum'll let her! And he and Todd have become good mates — Todd comes back home most weekends, and drives out here, but he's had to stay in Roma this week. His Dad bought him his own ute, an old Falcon, and he's so proud of that old truck! I'm not supposed to know, but he's been letting Michael drive it around the property — not that it would bother me, but you know what kids are, they like to have their guilty secrets!

Mike's been working with the boys some of the time here — they're showing him how to build fences, and taking him along when they've been bringing in some of the beasts for sale. He's getting quite good on a horse now — doesn't fall off very often! And they tell me he's a help, seems to enjoy the work — Alby sounds quite impressed. I think he thought his cousin would be a bit of a liability, get in the way — my boy isn't one to come out with unearned praise, so if he says he's doing all right, he means it. I'm quite happy for the boy to stay here as long as he likes, Steve — if you want him to go to college next year, that'll start in September, I guess? He can stay here until then, if you and Ellie are happy about it. If you want him back, on the other hand, just say so and we'll frog-march him to the plane! He seems to be really happy here, so it might be a bit of a struggle! Harrie and I are planning to take a few days off next week and take him up to Longreach, across the outback, and maybe a bit further up towards the channel country, show him what the real wild bush is like.

Otherwise, life here's pretty normal — Freddie's back in college now, and Susie and Brett are doing fine. They couldn't make the party in the end because he was somewhere up the Top End with the truck, but he's not working this week, hence our trip up there to see them. Sam and Ginny are good, too — he's doing really well now, got a couple of other fellas working for him, and they just love it down there on the coast. Jerry's been a bit crook, had a bad stomach, but he's getting over it now — too many years of living on steak and beans, probably! He's taken a shine to young Michael, too, spends hours sitting and talking to him, reminiscing about his time here. And the boy's been only too happy to help while he's been ill, taking meals to him and the like. That's a good kid you've got there!

Not much else to tell you, I guess — give our good wishes to everyone back home, and don't worry about that boy! He's having a great time, and we're happy to have him.

All the best

Mike.

October 23rd 1979

Dear Mike and Harrie,

Thanks for your letter — it's good to know Michael is okay and enjoying himself with you all out there! I hope, as you say, he really is being useful and not just a liability? He is a good boy, really — I just wish he'd sort himself out and stop his Dad getting so fed up with him!

Things here are much the same — Billy is working hard to get the Eagle fitted out, and we're expecting the Illustrious to be delivered early next month. They're nice looking boats — at least I think so! Steve doesn't like them much, he says they're strange, and I suppose after the old boats like the Albert they are a bit different — they have very long upswept fore-ends, and bars that sort of loop back up to the front corners of the cabin which are meant to protect them if anyone runs them into a bridge. It seems like a good idea to me — we got the Ruby back once with a cabin corner stove in when that had happened! — but Steve doesn't like the way it makes them look. And of course they have big open decks at the back where you steer them — he doesn't like that either! But it's much better for the people who hire them, they can all be together while someone's steering, and as they're meant for families that's a good thing.

You've started something now! After your letter, we got to talking one evening, about the old days on the boats. At least Steve and his Dad did! Bill told us all about that night he and Billy pulled you out of the cut – I knew it had happened, but not the whole story. And then they got on to talking about some of the sadder things that happened – I knew Carrie and Josh had lost their parents in an accident – but to see them drowned when the boat capsized! No wonder he took so long to get over it, poor kid. And Stevie still gets upset if he talks about his little brother – he still feels that he should have been able to save him, but Heaven knows how he could have done! He gives you all the credit for keeping an eye on him when that happened, for being there with him, did you know that? And what happened to the Beechey family in the freeze of 1947 – that was just awful! But we had a good laugh when Bill pulled Stevie's leg about him trying to turn that lock round on you – he actually got quite embarrassed about it! Blames me for distracting him, even if I was nowhere around at the time! I think what you said to him is etched on his memory: 'If you turn that lock around on me, Stevie Hanney, you'll be learning to swim in it!'

And we've had our laughs recently too – Steve told you about the man with the weed-hatch, didn't he? And there was the Royal Navy officer and his family – they hadn't been on the canal before, and he was used to big ships as first lieutenant on a destroyer. When they set off, he untied the boat, and threw the lines onto the bank! Luckily, Billy managed to catch him and tell him they needed to take them with them if they wanted to be able to moor up anywhere – he went off looking rather shame-faced, poor fellow! And then we had the man, a few months ago, who was obviously used to being in charge – they came back to the wharf with him standing on the fore-deck, waving and shouting directions to his poor wife who was steering – she got all flustered and forgot to stop! He ended up right over the fore-end onto the towpath when she hit the side. Didn't say much more, after that!

Looking back, even on the few years I had with Steve on the cut, they were good times, for the most part, weren't they? Hard work, often, but there was that feeling of freedom, travelling the countryside, and of independence. I think we were very lucky, later, the way things have worked out – most of the old boaters must have had to find work in factories or things like that. But we're still on the canal, even if it is in a very different way! And doing very well, if I'm honest.

Everyone here is well – Grace is rapidly getting to be the 'public face' of the business! She's kind of taken over as receptionist and chief telephone-answerer, and seems to be really enjoying it. She's a pretty gregarious sort of girl, always gets on well with people, so I suppose it suits her. That lad she was going out with dumped her a few weeks ago, and I think she was more upset than she let on – but she's getting over it now. Bill soldiers on the same as ever – he's amazing, really for his age! Still loves getting out on the Albert, and he's very much taken young Martin under his wing; I think there's some kind of trouble at home, but the boy won't talk about it. He's a nice kid, and seems to have really taken to helping Bill with the trip-boat.

Billy's fine, working hard as I said, and Sylvie's very well although she had a bad time after falling in to the front well of one of the boats – I told you about that, didn't I? Didn't break anything, but she got badly bruised, took ages to get over it. Their kids are all okay, at least as far as we know! Young Bill's not the best at keeping in touch, but he and Alison were fine the last we heard. Emily and Danny are fine, and their kids are okay, growing fast! Vi's still loving the teaching in Northampton – it's a big all-girls grammar school, supposed to be one of the best in the country. And Linda's at college now, of course, enjoying herself as far as we know!

I think that's about all! Not much news, really. I hope everything is okay with you all? Look after our boy, won't you, and if he does get to be a nuisance just send him home! Give him our love – the same to you all, of course, and tell Ginny it's time we had a letter from them, if you hear from her!

All my love,

Ellie.

November 4th 1979

Hi Steve, Ellie

Just a quick note to keep you up to date! Michael's been here two months now, and it sounds like he's really liking the Aussie lifestyle. Things here are pretty laid back, I guess, after the UK, no-one seems to be in a rush, not here in the bush anyhow, and that seems to suit him down to the ground. I think what I'm trying to say is that I'm not sure you're going to get him back at all — how would you both feel if he decided he wants to stay here permanently? Australia is still crying out for people, especially young ones with time and abilities to give something to the country, so there'd be no problem here if he does.

He hasn't said anything about it — but he doesn't need to! You can see it in his eyes, in his manner, Harrie's felt the same for a while — I think she spotted it before I did. She and I had a talk about it the other day while he was out fencing with the boys,

224

and we're both happy for him to stay here, at least as long as he might want to be a part of Marloo Creek, if things do go that way. We've got the room for him — with Freddie at college, and planning to apply to the RFDS once he's qualified, and Susie away with her own family, we've got the space here in the house. He's been using Susie's old room, and he could have it permanently if it comes to it. The work he's been doing here has been just for his bed and board, so far, but he seems to be enjoying it, and he's fitted in well with the other boys, doesn't seem bothered about taking orders from Alby when they're working, or from Kurt — he's a Swedish guy who's kind of Alby's understudy, sort of a foreman I guess you'd say. If he stays, I'll pay him the same rate as the other hands, of course — but if he wants to go and find other work, that's okay too. It's his life, after all!

And we reckon there's more going on with him and Anna than either of them's admitting. She spends a lot of time with him, here at home and out together — they go riding most weekends, and they've been into Mitchell to barbies with the town kids a few times, stayed with Carrie at the pub. I've been teaching him to drive, and he's borrowed the old ute a couple of times to take her out. Harrie's a bit worried about our girl, after all she's only fifteen, but then she's a sensible kid, she's not going to let anything stupid happen.

The trip up to Longreach was just great, we all had a grand time of it! Brett and Susie made us all very welcome, even if it was a bit of a squeeze in their house — Anna had to share with little Vanessa, because they've only got the four bedrooms. It's a nice house, on a half-acre plot, and they're talking about extending it one day — but they've no need to as yet. Even when little Adam's in his own room, they'll still have the one spare — but I reckon there'll be more grandkids on the way in time, so I guess then they'll have to! We took the week out, left Alby in charge back home, and took

Mike right out into the wild bush — had a couple of days in Boulia, and went out to take a look at parts of the Burke and Wills trail. It's incredible country out there, and I think he was pretty impressed — I know we were! We don't get to see the grandkids that often, so that was great for Harrie and me, too.

We packed Mike off to stay with Sam and Ginny a couple of weeks later, down on the coast — he came back full of beans, but with a badly bruised arm and shoulder. The daft sod had fallen off a surfboard, trying to impress the girls! He's fine now, pretty much over the stiffness — Anna was all sympathy, fussing over him, until he kept going on about all the pretty girls he'd met on the beach! But I think she's forgiven him now.

Freddie's sitting his final exams, reckons he's doing okay — I guess we'll find out in time! And Alby and Lesley are talking about making it official, at last! We could be planning a wedding for the autumn, Harrie reckons. Jerry's been a bit crook again, his tummy's still playing him up from time to time — I'm taking him in to see the nurse in town tomorrow, just to play safe. He's about 75, we reckon — I think he's a bit like the old boaters, not too sure himself just when he was born! And any records are back in Ireland, of course.

I reckon that's about all to tell you right now — let us know what you think about Michael's future, and we'll try and find out just what he's thinking!

All the best,
Mike.

November 15th 1979

Mike – thank you for your letter. Talk about conflicting thoughts! If Michael wanted to stay there, to live in Australia, I suppose we would support him – but this business of him and Anna just isn't on! Mike, they're cousins – it's not right! You've got to put a stop to it, before it gets out of hand. If it comes to it, you'll have to put him on the plane home, whether he likes it or not. I'm sorry, but this has really upset me.

Steve's away at the moment, staying in London for a meeting of the hire-boat operators association – I'm sure he'd back me up on this. I don't want to spoil anyone's fun, if that's all it is, but we can't let it go anywhere beyond that, I'm sure you can see that?

I'm going to drop this note in the post straight away – I'll write later with the usual news and so on, but I'm too worried for that at the moment. Do write back and let me know what's happening, please?

In haste,

Ellie

November 25th 1979

Dear Ellie,

You are worrying about nothing! I do understand your reaction to the idea of Mike and Anna together — but stop and think about it? Yes, we always talk about your kids and ours as cousins — but they're not! Not in reality.

I've always thought of Steve as if he was my brother, we've always been that close, I guess — but we're not actually related. He's a Hanney — I was born a Thompson, remember? Not from the boats at all. And Harrie's a Caplin, so our children and yours have no actual blood relationship at all.

I hope I haven't offended you, pointing this out — I know there are sensibilities about such things, but they really aren't justified in this case! I hope, rather, that I've put your mind at rest. I have dropped a hint to both of them to cool it a bit, partly until I hear from you again to know if their relationship, if indeed it becomes one, has your blessing, and partly because our Anna is still only fifteen, and we don't want her getting too carried away until she's a bit older. We don't want her to make any mistakes — not that I'm suggesting Mike might be anything but an excellent husband for someone, in time! Please don't worry, we'll keep an eye on them anyway — but if it does develop into a romance, I can't see any reason to put the brakes on it, given that they are both a bit on the young side.

On to other news — Alby and Lesley have decided they are going to get married, and we're planning for sometime in March. We'll hold it here, with a visiting priest to officiate, and a big party after! We seem to be having a big do every six months just lately — first my fiftieth, then the effort for Harrie and Mike and the rest two months ago, and now the wedding. I don't suppose you and Steve could make it out here? It would be so good to see you again — but we do understand you've got a business to run, just like us, and that takes priority.

The only blot on the horizon is Jerry — the nurse thinks he's got something serious with his stomach, possibly cancer. I ran him in to Roma, to the hospital, last week, and they did a load of tests, X-rays and things, and we're waiting for the results. He'll quite probably have to go there for an op at some stage, but we're hoping it's not too bad. He's great old boy, so much part of the family after all these years, and we're all worried about him.

Everyone else is okay — Sam and Ginny and the girls are coming here for Christmas this year, and Brett and Susie are hoping to join us as well, but he might be working right up to Christmas Eve, so they might have to come down later. Carrie and Davey will be busy with the pub over the holiday of course, but I'm sure we'll be popping into town to see them at some stage!

Not much else to tell — take care, and don't worry about the kids! I'll keep you up to speed with any developments — but do drop me a line back, let me know that you're happy about everything?

All our love,

Mike.

December 5th 1979

Dear Mike, Harriet

    I feel like a complete fool! I dashed that letter off to you without stopping to think it out, and now I owe you all an apology, especially the two kids. Please forgive my stupidity?

    Steve came back from his conference the day after I'd sent it – I told him all about it, showed him your letter, the bit about Michael and Anna, and the rotten swine just burst out laughing! He sat me down and explained it all, the same as you did in your letter – and of course you're both quite right. I cannot help thinking of you all as family, and I forget the background to it all. So – I'm sorry I went off half-cocked! I should have stopped to think about it before putting pen to paper – forgive me? And tell Michael and Anna that if they do think that much of each other, it's fine with us. Just ask them to hold their horses until they're a bit older, please?

    We had our own drama here, the other week. You remember I told you about the young lad, Martin, who's been helping Bill with the Albert a lot this year? He turned up on our doorstep one night, practically in tears, poor kid – we took him in, but he wouldn't tell us what was wrong. Steve got his Dad to come and talk to the boy, and he managed to get it out of him. I'd suspected he had trouble at home for a while – it turns out it's all down to his Mum's boyfriend. She's divorced from his Dad, a long time ago, and this new fellow of hers sounds like a complete swine. He's not only been knocking her and the kid about, but he's started making advances to the boy, tried to get his trousers down more than once. He's only fourteen, for goodness' sake! Poor little beggar – he couldn't stand it there any longer, ran out, and then realized he didn't know where to go. I suppose we're the only people he could think of who might help him.

Anyhow – he's staying in Michael's room at the moment! I don't know what we're going to do with him in the long run, but we couldn't send him back to that nightmare, could we? Bill thinks the world of the kid, he's really taken him under his wing, and Martin seems so much happier over the last couple of weeks. I've been running him in to school every day, and we explained to the head teacher what had happened, and she's very supportive, keeping an eye on him while he's there. It doesn't look as if his mother cares much about him, she's made no effort to get him back – we're assuming she'd rather have the boyfriend. So for the time being at least, we're saddled with him! He's no trouble, bless him, a nice kid really – surprising perhaps, given what he's been going through. Even Grace has kind of adopted him as a spare brother, now she hasn't got Michael to boss around!

Things here go on much the same, otherwise – the two new boats are coming along nicely, will be ready in plenty of time for next season, and bookings are beginning to come in. We're hoping for an even better year – the demand just seems to grow all the time! We're having to put the prices up year by year, which is a worry, but people still keep coming – the cost of fuel is going up all the time, and insurance is getting to be expensive too. We don't have many claims, but some of the other operators have had some bad ones, and I suppose that scares the insurance companies!

Everyone here is well – Emmie had the kids poorly with the Chicken Pox not long ago, but they're getting over it now. And young Bill was on the phone the other day – it seems that Alison is expecting! I don't think they'd planned this, the way he was talking about it, but you could tell that he's over the moon! Another grandchild for Billy and Sylvie – he loves his grandchildren, but I'm not sure he likes to be reminded that he's getting older – how is it possible that the time is passing so quickly? Stevie will be fifty next year – I'm forty-eight! I can't be, can I? I guess you all feel the same? It's great to watch the kids grow up, but it's sad, somehow, too, isn't it? There are times I'd give anything to have a little Michael climb on my lap and give me a big kiss again! He'd squash me if he tried it now...

Enough of the nostalgia! Give our love to all 'down under', and tell Michael we're thinking of him and missing him. If he does decided he wants to stay in Australia, we will of course back him all the way – but it will be a wrench, as you will understand.

With our love,

Ellie.

PS – parcel and cards in the post any time! Have a great Christmas.

E.

December 16th 1979

Hi Steve, Ellie and all!

Merry Christmas! I guess you'll just about get this letter in time — I hope our parcel will make it, Harrie was a bit late getting it all together. We included a little something for your lodger, he sounds like a kid who needs a few people to think about him! Is he still with you — what are you going to do about him?

Michael asked me to send you all his love — I think with Christmas coming he's realizing that he does miss you all, at least a bit! We should have a great time here with all the family around, so he won't have time to think about it once the holiday starts. And he and I sat down and had a long talk a few days ago — he is very torn about what he wants to do. Deep down, he really wants to stay here — he says he loves it in Aus — but at the same time he misses his family, and I think there's an element of feeling that he's let you down somehow. He says he really ought to be with you, to be a part of Steve's company, but I can see that that isn't what he wants for himself. He got quite upset about it. For my part, I think he'd do very well here if he stayed — there a certain wildness about the kid that fits in so well with our lifestyle, especially out here in the bush, a kind of laid-back attitude that is very Australian. Mind you, he's perhaps picked that up since he's been here! Everyone here likes the boy — Alby seems to have adopted him almost as another little brother, and the bunkhouse boys all get on with him. He's adapted to the Aussie sense of humour very well, doesn't get wound up when people rib him but gives as good as he gets — that's something that gives a lot of Poms trouble here! So we would be only too pleased to keep him, if you were agreeable. I know how difficult that decision will be for you — I know how I would feel if Freddie suddenly decided to go back to England. It's a long way away! And Michael is so much younger. To be selfish about it, too, I'm afraid if he does go home we'll be losing Anna at some time in the future — those two seem to be more and more inseparable as time goes by. It could still come to nothing, of course — but somehow I doubt it! Sorry to dump such a worry on you over Christmas!

On to other news — Alby and Les have decided on March 29th for the wedding, so once Christmas is over we'll be busy organizing that do. Should be quite a party! Her folks from Toowoomba will be there of course, and I guess a lot of her friends as well as all of ours, so the place could get a bit crowded. Freddie's as nervous as a kitten at the moment, waiting for his results — he's applied to the RFDS for a job, and one or two of the hospitals around here in case they don't want him. Susie thinks she's pregnant again — another grandkid on the way! Makes you feel old — I know how Billy feels, it makes you aware that you aren't as young as you might like anymore. We're really looking forward to seeing them over the holiday — Brett's got the week after

Christmas off, so they're driving down Christmas morning and staying for a while. It's great having grandkids, you ought to try it! You can have fun with them, and then give them back before they get to be hard work — it's much better than kids of your own! Carrie and Davey and the boys are all good — Kyle's enjoying the air force, put in for flying training. The idea of my nephew in a few million dollars worth of jet is a bit scary! And we see quite a bit of Todd these days — he often drives out to see Michael when he's home over the weekend, and the two of them are thick as thieves!

We got the results of Jerry's tests — he does have cancer of the stomach, but they're saying it's not as bad as it sounds, they've spotted it in good time so he's got a good chance. He goes into Roma to the hospital next week for the op, and we're hoping to have him back in time for Christmas. He won't be able to take much solid food then, so we're all pulling his leg about stuffing ourselves with turkey and pud while he has to sit and watch! Poor bastard! I'm going to drive him there in the Chrysler, and Mike's insisting on coming along, bless the kid. So it'll be the four of us — I'm not even going to try to stop Anna coming! All of our kids think the world of Jerry, he's been like a kind of uncle to them all these years, and they're worried about him even if they don't want to show it.

Not much else to tell, I guess — take care of yourselves, and have a great Christmas.

With all our love,
Mike.

January 6th 1980

Hello Mikey, Harrie and all!

I hope you all had a super Christmas and New Year? We had a grand time, the usual family gathering of course – Just us here for Christmas Day, Steve, Grace and Bill, and young Martin, but then Billy and Sylvie came over for Boxing Day, with Violet and Linda. We all went to them for New Year, and young Bill and Alison were there too – it was great to meet his girl at last! We saw Emily and Danny and their kids one day in between as well – they came to us for dinner one day. It did seem odd without Michael here, and I think Stevie was missing his boy, but I'm sure he will have had a great time with you all!

About Martin - it seems like we've got ourselves another kid! It's a long story, but I'll try to keep it brief: Back before Christmas, we had the local Children's Services around. The headmistress at his school had got in touch with them – I suppose it was the right thing for her to do. It seems they already had had some dealings with the family, but obviously had no idea just how bad things were. Martin didn't want to talk to the lady, he said they'd been to see him before and they were a waste of time. Bill took the woman into his sitting-room and told her all of what Martin had told him, about his mother's boyfriend – I'm not sure she believed him, but eventually we got Martin to confirm it all. Her reaction was to insist on taking him away and putting him in a children's home – that sounds horribly familiar, doesn't it? It brought back your story of how they tried to snatch Ginny away from you all those years ago! Martin was obviously upset at that idea, but didn't know what else to suggest – he doesn't want to go home at any price. The Council woman was getting very impatient with him, telling him he had no choice and had to go with her. That was when I opened my big mouth!

I said if it came to it, he could stay with us and we'd look after him. You should have seen the kid's face – and then he burst into tears, poor little beggar! The Council woman didn't like that suggestion at all, but in the end she gave up because he clearly wasn't going to go along with her ideas. Anyway, the upshot of it is that they've agreed now that he can stay here as long as we make sure he goes to school and so on, and they'll come and check up on him every couple of weeks. They sent someone around to the house for the rest of his things, and I gather the mother basically said good riddance to him – poor little sod, what a life he must have had there! He's a different kid now, so cheerful and full of beans.

I'm just a bit concerned about what Michael's going to think – he's our son, and we love him to pieces and I wouldn't want him to think that this boy's taking his place in our affections. But if he really wants to make a life for himself there in Australia, having Martin here will be a help to us, I think! With him to worry about, we perhaps won't miss our boy quite so much, if you see what I mean? But he's not ours – Michael is our boy, and he always will be, wherever he is in the world. If he stays with you, we are going to miss him terribly – but tell him that we love him very much, and we will be happy with whatever he decides. If his future is out there, then that is what he must do. And we will get to see him again – maybe we'll come out to see you all, one day, or he can always fly home for a holiday.

Everyone here's well – we had a long chat with Joe on the phone the other day, and their family are all okay too. His back is still bad, but he's managing okay, still driving part-time. Had a letter from Ginny the other day, with the latest pictures of their girls – pretty little things, aren't they both? It's about time you sent us some new photos!

Anyway – look after yourselves, all of you, and give our love to all, especially that errant boy of ours! Tell him write to us himself, lazy beggar!

With all our love,

Ellie.

January 20th 1980

Dear Mum and Dad, and Gracie,

Auntie Harriet's been on at me to write to you myself, and I suppose she's right! I've never been good at writing letters, have I – remember all the times you had to keep on at me to write my thank-you's after Christmas!

Anyway Mum, Dad – I know Uncle Mikey has been telling you all about my ideas of staying here in Australia. I know how much you must hate that idea – but it _is_ what I really want to do. This is such an amazing place, Mum – I can't really describe it, but it just makes me feel at home, somehow. And everyone is so great, the whole attitude to life is so much easier, there doesn't seem to be the same kind of pressure, that sort rushing around there always is back home.

Uncle Mikey has offered me a job here on the station, at least to start with, and I so much want to do that! He's said he'll send me to the same Agri college that Alby went to, if I like – we've missed this year's entries, so it'd have to be next year now. It's a three-year course, but I'd come out a certificated agriculturalist, and then I could get work anywhere in Queensland, or anywhere else for that matter! What do you think?

But I can't help feeling that if I do that, I'm letting you and Dad down. And part of me knows how much I'll miss you both, and Gracie and Uncle Billy and Auntie Sylv and everyone, not to mention Granddad! – it'll be difficult, too, and I know that you'd rather have me at home. But sometime soon, I suppose I'd be moving out anyway, wouldn't I? Getting a job, maybe going away somewhere, so this isn't really so much different, is it? It won't be like just up the road, and we won't be able to pop in and see each other very easily, but – I know how much Dad's wanted me to make up my mind what I want to do, and I suppose now I have, haven't I? It's just not what any of us expected. I really want to do this – please say it's all right?

If I can't start college until this time next year, I think what I should do is come home for a bit. That way, I could be with you all for a while, maybe help around the place during the summer, with the turn-arounds and so on. And if Dad would maybe pay me a bit for my work, it'd let me save up a bit towards the college fees so that Uncle Mikey doesn't have to pay everything. And it would give me time to really think things over – I don't think I'm going to change my mind, but maybe

I'd see things with a different perspective, get a clearer idea of just what I do want.

One thing I want to get my head around is Anna, and I think it'd do both of us good to have some time apart. She's absolutely amazing, Mum – so pretty, and bright and clever, and great fun just to be with! I think I'm in love with her – I know she's only fifteen, but I think she loves me too. But if we don't see each other for a while, a few months, maybe we can both look at it more calmly, if you see what I mean? If we still feel the same afterwards, then maybe it is right, don't you think?

We've been out riding today, had a great time – we went up the creek, out into the open bush. It's amazing out there – there's just no-one there, for miles and miles, and you could be the only two people in the world! We got caught in the rain, but it's so warm it just doesn't matter — once it stops, your clothes just dry again in the sun. I love riding now — you should have seen me at first! I couldn't stay on a horse for love nor money, had the bruises for ages! But now I've got the hang of it, it's just great — out there, you get such a feeling of freedom. The country just goes on for ever, and there's so much sky over your head — that sounds silly — you have to see it to know what I mean! And being there just feels so right — especially if Anna's with me.

Anyway, Mum, Dad — write back, tell me what you think. Give my love to Gracie, and to everyone. I love you all, and I'll see you soon, one way or the other!

All my love,

Michael.

January 22nd 1980

Hi Steve, Ellie

　　Michael's written to you I know — but we owe you all a letter after Christmas anyway! Everything went off as expected, a grand time was had by all — Brett and Susie had a few days here and it was good to see them. He's doing well, still driving big rigs around the Top End mostly, got his Roadtrain ticket now. The kids are wonderful, and the next one's due in June! Sam and Ginny were here too, so we had to shoe-horn people in, but it was great to have such a big do, with a couple of the boys in the bunkhouse staying over too. The kids, Ginny's and Susie's, all slept in sleeping-bags out on the veranda! We had a day in Mitchell with Carrie and Davey too, and Kyle was on leave from his training, so that was good, all of us playing cricket in the backyard. My batting definitely improves with the addition of beer!

We had a real shock on Christmas Day
– Anna came down in a dress! I don't think
I've seen her in one for years – and she
looked so lovely. I think your Michael being
there might have had something to do with
it! She's <u>always</u> in jeans and a shirt, so it
came as quite a surprise.

Jerry's doing fine now, he'll be back
on proper food before long! The op went
okay, the docs reckon he'll make a full
recovery, but they had to take away quite a
bit of his stomach. No more steak and eggs
for Jerry, poor sod! He's got to stick to an
easier diet now, but I reckon we'll have a job
keeping him to it.

About Michael – we had another long
talk about a week ago. I've told him if he
wants to stay here, he's got a job on the
property if he wants it. And if he does, I'll
send him to college to study agri – he might
as well get some kind of quali's, and he'll be
more use around here if he knows what he's
doing! He's talking about going back to the
UK for a while – he can't start college now

for a year, anyway — and I think that's sensible of him. It'll give him a chance to think things out, make sure he's sure of what he wants to do. And it'll make him and Anna face up to just how strong their relationship is. He says he's in love with her, but they're both very young, her especially, and if they have a bit of time apart we'll see if it holds up or if they drift off and find other attractions. Anna is very reticent about how she feels, with me anyway, but Harrie says that she's told her she loves him — but we'll see! If it works out, I have no worries — I'd be proud to have Mike as a son-in-law, he's a fine young fella.   We talked about your spare kid, too — he's rather pleased about him, on the quiet, I think. He didn't say as much, but I think he's feeling that if you've got this other lad to look after, you might not miss him so much.   And he's keen to meet him again, remembers him from when he used to cycle over there — I think he wants to see what it's like to have a younger brother! How is all that going now — is the boy still happy to be with you? You can't help thinking that he must miss his mother, even if she sounds like a pretty awful parent, especially over Christmas. I'm glad he liked the Aussie shirts we sent him — we had to guess at the size! Harrie was very touched that he took the trouble to write to us to say thank you.

Not much else to tell you — the summer's been pretty average, so far, quite a bit of rain so the creek's pretty high but not enough to be a worry — but this is the typhoon season, so we could get wetter yet! Harrie keeps the larder well filled every year, in case we get stranded like a few years back when the roads got washed out, but it doesn't happen often. Thirty-one degrees today, nice and warm, and the sun's shining at the moment — how's your winter weather?

With our love,

Mike.

February 7th 1980

Dear Michael,

It was good to get a letter from you, even if it did make your mother cry! Don't take that the wrong way - you know how emotional your Mum can get sometimes. I'm not sure if she was touched to hear from you direct instead of getting your news from Uncle Mike or upset at your plans!

We sat down the other night and had a long talk about you, son. And we're both agreed, if your future is in Australia then that is where you must be. You are our son, come what may, and we will be behind you whatever you decide to do - that doesn't sound right! What I mean to say is that we love you more than I can tell you, and we want whatever is best for you, for your life, even if it means that you will be half way around the world from us.

We think you are right to come home for a while - as you say, it will give you a chance to look at things away from the situation, to have a different view of your ideas and plans. Your Mum has promised not to try and talk you out of it, so don't worry about that! And it will give both you and Anna the time to think about yourselves, to see if what you feel for each other is strong enough to stand up to a bit of time apart. I don't know what he's said to you, but Uncle Mike has told us that, in time, he would be delighted if you and Anna did get together - but he is concerned that she is still very young. So are you, if it comes to it, young man! Seventeen is really too young to know your own mind in matters of love and marriage - we hope you'll hold your horses for a while? Uncle Mike isn't going to let you get too carried away anyway, with Anna only fifteen!

Grace says she hopes you'll stay there, that it'll be good to have you out of her way permanently! But we all know she'll miss you terribly, in fact - she and your Mum had a quiet little weep together the other day that I'm not supposed to know about. Uncle Billy says good on you, go for it, and your cousin Bill is very taken with the idea - over Christmas, he and Alison were talking about the idea of emigrating themselves! And your Granddad says to tell you to do whatever is right for you. He did admit he's going to miss you - he wouldn't ever tell you, but he thinks the world of you, Michael. And Martin is keen to see you again - I expect Uncle Mike has told you he's living with us now? Your Mum will tell you all about it when we see you. He's a nice kid, and we're happy to have him here - but I don't want you to think he's taking your place. You are our son, and you always will be!

What I'm trying to say, son, is put your mind at rest. You haven't let us down, far from it! I'm so pleased that you have found your future. I'm so proud of you, boy - you're a fine young fellow, and you're going to go on to be a man I will be even more proud to call my son in the future.

I expect you'll stay there for Alby's wedding? It would be a shame to miss that, it sounds as though they really know how to party out there! If you come home in April, for the summer, I'll put you to work around the place! You can help Auntie Sylv with the turn-arounds, and Uncle Billy on the mechanical stuff - you might even learn something useful for life in the outback! And of course I'll pay you for what you do, the same as anyone else, as long as you promise to save it towards your college. We'll send you the money for your air fare, if you let us know how much.

Your Mum and I are so much looking forward to seeing you - and when you go back in the autumn we'll give you a proper send-off!

Take care of yourself, Michael; give our love to Uncle Mike and Auntie Harriet, and to your cousins out there. If you see Uncle Sam and Auntie Ginny, say hello for us and tell them your Mum's going to write to them any day now!

Everyone here sends you their love, and we're all looking forward to seeing you soon;

With our love,

Mum and Dad.

Interlude

1980

October 6ᵗʰ 1980

Dear Mike and Harrie,

I hope the boy arrived in one piece? We had quite a party to send him off, and I think he was still a bit thick-headed when we poured him onto the plane!

We've had the best year ever with the boats, Mike - I have to pinch myself to believe the state of our bank balance! I think the bank manager feels a bit the same - he's been trying to persuade me to expand the business, to think about opening another base somewhere else around the canals. Some of the other operators have more than one, some of them quite a number! An outfit called Black Prince Boats are all over the place - but not too close to us, thank goodness. We've talked about it, Ellie, Dad, Billy and James and myself - James is the only one who was quite keen to do it, the rest of us feel that we're doing very well as we are. I'm afraid that to have a second place to run would be stretching ourselves a bit too much, and it would make our lives a lot more complicated. I don't think the extra cost would translate that easily into more profit - there'd be the rent for another old wharf or similar, and we'd never get it at the rate we pay here! Plus more boats, more staff, more insurance - and the mental burden of overseeing it all. Anyway, we've decided just to continue slowly building things up here.

Two more new boats on order for '81 - that's 23 altogether now! It's enough to be coping with - we try to refurbish a few of the older ones every year, to keep them looking clean and smart, and attractive to the hirers. It pays off - we get so much repeat business, and a lot of referrals from customers too, so we must be doing something right!

I'm planning to refit the Albert this winter, too - update it, and modernize the bar area. People expect a bit more comfort and luxury now than they did when we first converted it! Dad's overseeing that job, with young Martin peering over his shoulder - that boy's becoming quite proprietorial about your old motor! He steers it most of the time now, when he's not in school. He's turning out to be a really good lad, and Ellie and I have thought about trying to adopt him, but we can't because his mother won't sign the papers. She's not interested in the kid, just being bloody-minded! But he's ours in all but name, and we're so pleased to have him. He and Michael got on famously all summer - Mike said he's really pleased that we've got him too, he feels a bit less guilty about leaving us now!

I guess that brings me to the point, doesn't it? I suppose, in effect Mike, I'm handing my son over to you - and you cannot imagine how difficult that is. But he's eighteen now, his own man, and if he wants to live in Australia, it's his decision to make. All his mother and I can do is support him. But it is going to be so hard, knowing that it will probably be years before we see him again.

We were both astounded at the change in him when he got back here - we sent you a rather vague, directionless boy, and we got back a fit, tanned, self-assured young man - how did you do it? He was always my son, and I've always been proud of him in my own way, but now he is a fellow any man would be delighted to call his son - tall and handsome and self-confident - if you have half as much pride and joy in Alby and Freddie, then I am truly happy for you, Mike.

It was great to have him here for his eighteenth - he organised the party - I think he's been learning from you Aussies! We all had a grand time - I'm sure he'll tell you all about it! And we had a smaller do for him the night before he left, just the family, here in the house. Ellie had a bit too much wine, and ended up crying on his shoulder - you should have seen his face! Somewhere between embarrassed and upset, trying desperately not to cry himself. Not done, if you're eighteen, crying on your Mum's shoulder. But we were all in tears before we'd finished, even Martin! He's really adopted Mike as his big brother. Dad was putting on a brave face, but we all know how much he loves his grandson - and at his age, he must have been wondering if he'll ever see him again. I don't want to sound morbid, but you'll understand.

Anyway, Mike, take care of my boy, make him work hard and keep him on his toes! And remind him from time to time that we're still here, and the occasional letter would be nice...

I hope you're all well, out there, enjoying the springtime - we're plunging steadily into another cold, drab winter! Give our love to all the family - thank Susie for the pictures, little Emmett looks like a cute kid, tell her Ellie will write back very soon.

With our love,
Steve and Ellie.

October 19th 1980

Dear Steve and Ellie,

Just a quick reply to say that Michael is safely back with us and settling in as though he's always belonged here! He's changed, even in the few months you had him back — more confident again, very much the young man, so different from the diffident boy who arrived here a year ago! We're delighted to have him back, no-one more so than Anna — it seems that their feelings for each other have survived the separation. I think the last six months have cost me a fortune in ink and stamps! Not to say phone calls...

I know how you must be feeling, both of you. But as you say Steve, he's a man now, and has to make up his own mind about his future. He will make a real success of life here, I'm certain, he has the right approach to do well in Aus, whether in the long run he stays with Marloo Creek or moves on elsewhere. But he's going to be an asset to me and the station as long as we've got him, I'm sure! I'm thinking of taking a step back sometime soon, leaving more of the running of the place to Alby — and if Michael wants to be his right-hand man, in time, that would be fair dinkum! I've enrolled him for Agri college, starting after Christmas, so he might know what he's doing in a few years' time, too.

We had a barbie here for friends and family, to welcome him back, and everyone turned up — Carrie and Davey and Todd, Sam and Ginny and the girls — only Susie couldn't make it, little Adam's been a bit crook and she didn't want to subject him to the journey, and of course Emmett's only four months old. But Brett turned up out of the blue, complete with about seventy tons of truck! He'd swung a trip down around this way with a B-double and made a bit of a diversion, as he put it — only about a hundred miles! I don't know what his boss would make of it, if he knew! Freddie drove over from Roma — he's doing fine there in the hospital, working all hours but really enjoying it. Still hoping to get into the RFDS in time — they did tell him to re-apply once he'd got a couple of years of experience under his belt.

Harrie and me are going to take a break next week, go up to see Susie and the baby again, and the grandkids of course! We'll take Mike (and Anna — just try and keep those two apart!) to see them, and maybe come back via the coast and Ginny's place for a day or two. We've got a couple of weeks before the next big stock sale here, so Alby and the boys can look after things okay. Anyway, rest assured that your boy's fine and enjoying life — I'll get some new pics of the kids and write again soon.

Michael says to send you all his love, and he promises to write to you himself very soon...!

All our best,
Mike.

Interlude

1984

November 25th 1984

My very dear Mike and Harrie,

We're all back safe and sound in the UK! I'm home, and getting over the jet-lag slowly – Stevie picked us up from the airport yesterday, and we all slept for about 24 hours! It's an awful journey, isn't it? All that time on a plane – and I can't sleep when I'm travelling whatever I do. Michael and Anna crept down for breakfast, only to be presented with dinner, much to Grace's amusement! They're taking it easy in the lounge as I write this, looking half-asleep again.

Thank you all so much for all you've done – the wedding was the most wonderful affair, I wish Stevie could have been there with me! But I know you all understand – the business has to come first. Maybe I'll persuade him to go and visit you one day for himself – but I wouldn't hold your breath! I know he'd love to see you all again, but not if it means leaving his baby!

We're sending Michael and Anna off for their honeymoon proper the day after tomorrow. They're going to borrow the Jaguar, Steve's arranged insurance cover for them while they're here, and tour around Scotland – not where I'd choose to go this time of the year, but Michael is so keen to go there again and show Anna what it's like – he really loved the scout camps he went on there when he was a boy. When – I still find it hard to believe that my little boy is a grown man with a wife of his own! They are such a beautiful couple, aren't they? He's so handsome, tall like his granddad, and she's the loveliest girl – but then, perhaps I'm a bit biased!

Everyone here is fine – Steve and Billy are working as hard as ever, young Bill and Alison are still talking about emigrating with the children, thinking about New Zealand – tales of your climate have put them off Australia, as Al doesn't do hot weather! Emily and Danny and their two are all well, moved to Bromley now that he's working at the Victoria and Albert Museum. Vi is still in Northampton, head of PE there now, and Linda's enjoying her maths teaching in County Durham. Grace has moved to the town, got a nice little house there with her Edward, but no plans to get married yet - or for any kids! She's our secretary/booking clerk/receptionist/ dogsbody in the business now, very much the public face of Midland Canal Holidays! And Martin has grown into a fine young fellow – I'm so pleased we were able to take him in when we did, I dread to think what might have become of him if we hadn't. He effectively runs the Albert now, as skipper although Bill is still nominally in charge because he's too young to be captain officially! Bill soldiers on the same as ever – he just doesn't change! He's a fit and well as he ever was, I swear, although he must be about ninety years old. Still loves to be on the boat, talking to the customers whether they're a WI or a historical group or a stag party or a school outing! The girls in the occasional hen nights we get always love him – they can get awfully rude sometimes, and he just takes it in his stride, and they make a huge fuss of him! We've had to go and collect him from the wharf more than once, because they've been plying him with rum all night!

We're still doing very well, although the economy here has been on a bit of a roller-coaster for the last few years. I'm pleased we didn't try to get too big – some of the other companies are hurting now because they were over-committed, but we're plodding along, doing all right. Holding steady at 25 boats, and getting most of them out for a large part of the season – Steve's beginning to replace one or two of the oldest ones, but for the most part we just refurbish them to keep them sound and looking smart, and equipped the way people want today with TV's and microwave ovens and so on. And he said to tell you that they finally got the Blisworth Tunnel open again! Five years, it took them – but they've done a really amazing job. It turned out that the whole middle part of the tunnel was in real danger of collapsing, so they've effectively redug about seven hundred yards of it and relined it with concrete sections. It's quite a way from us here, of course, but it still affects our hirers – now the really ambitious ones can do what they call the London Ring! Down to Limehouse or Brentford on the Junction, up the Thames and back up the Oxford. We have one or two a year who want to do it – takes at least three weeks, so it makes for a nice long hire from our point of view!

That's enough for now – I'm going to stop writing before I fall asleep over my pen! Thank you again for everything, I really loved the time I had there with you all. Give my love to Sam and Ginny and the girls, to Carrie and Davey and their boys, and to all your kids – and give Jerry a big kiss for me! He's such a sweetie, isn't he?

With my love,

Ellie.

Epilogue

1987

Top Lock Wharf, Knowle, Warwickshire.

The Offices of Midland Canal Holidays Ltd:

Steven Hanney turned away from the window with a sigh and glanced at the calendar on his office wall: The twelfth of September, 1987: The season would be slowing down to its close over the next month, with just a surge of demand over the October school half-term holiday to round things off.

Saturday, and turn-around day for the fleet of hire-boats. The scene outside his window had been one of efficient, controlled chaos, as the teams of cleaners scurried from boat to boat and the yard men filled water and diesel tanks and pumped out toilets. The first of the week's new customers would be arriving at any moment — in fact, the murmur of voices through his partly-open office door suggested that they already had. But he had other things on his mind — two new boats to be built during the quiet winter months, the plans for them on his desk awaiting his approval — and the end-of-year accounts to be gone through with their accountant.

In the outer office, Grace Hanney looked up with a smile as another customer approached her desk:

'Good morning — can I help you?' The tall, well-built man in the expensive-looking raincoat with a broad-brimmed hat on his greying sandy hair gave her a cheerful smile; behind him, she quickly took in the others of his party — a lady who had to be his wife, and another couple, perhaps slightly younger, the woman probably his sister from her

276

looks. He addressed her in a clearly southern-hemisphere accent:

'G'day — yeh've got a boat booked fer us today.' He looked at the nameplate on her desk: 'You're Grace Hanney, are yeh?'

'I am — do I know you, Mr... ?' The man laughed:

'Yeh wouldn' remember me — but yer Dad will!' Grace smiled uncertainly at him as she got to her feet:

'He's in the office — shall I call him?'

'In there?' The man pointed to the door behind her.

'That's right, sir.' The man chuckled again:

'Then fergive me, Grace...' He stepped past her and paused by the partly-open door where he could not be seen from its far side, and raised his voice:

'Yew turn that lock round, Stevie 'Anney, 'n yeh'll be learnin' ter swim in it!'

In the office, Hanney's head snapped up, a look of utter disbelief on his face. That voice, those words – it couldn't be? He stood rooted to the spot for a moment, but then turned and snatched the door open, to be met with the huge grin and twinkling eyes of someone he hadn't seen for thirty years:

'Mikey? Mikey Baker! What the Hell are you doing here?' Michael laughed:

'Takin' a trip in one o' your boats!' The two stared at each other for a few more seconds – and then they were in each other's arms, laughing, slapping each other on the back. Grace stood at their side, realization dawning on her face as she watched her father in his astonished joy. She turned, to see the man's wife also watching, her face too split into a wide grin; and their other companions – his sister? And her husband? She picked up the booking form from her desk – what was the name? Marlow? Marlow! Of course – why

277

hadn't she spotted that? She looked up at the woman regarding her with an amused smile:

'Auntie Harriet?' The woman reached out and took her in her arms, kissed her on the cheek:

'Hello, Grace. It's good to meet yeh at last.' They stared into each other's eyes as Grace took in the sight of the Aunt she had never met. Then she looked at the other couple:

'Auntie Ginny?'

'Too right, Grace! It's real grand to see yeh – come here girl!' They embraced, and she caught the sparkling eye of the last member of the party over Ginny's shoulder:

'Uncle Sam?' The man nodded:

'S'roight, Grace. Good ter see yeh at last! Yeh're even prettier than yer pictures.' She laughed as he held her and gave her a kiss:

'Dad says you were always a charmer, Uncle Sam! It's amazing – it's just wonderful to see you all!'

Sam Caplin released her, to take her father's hand. Steve, still in the thrall of disbelief, shook it and then drew Sam also into a hug. He stared around at the visitors:

'Why didn't you let us know you were coming?' Michael laughed:

'We thought we'd keep it as a nice surprise for yeh!'

**If you've not read them, why not
try Geoffrey Lewis' most popular
stories to date?**

*The Michael Baker trilogy is set around
Britain's Canals in the days of the commercial
carrying trade. Beginning at the start of the
Second World War, the story carries us
through into the 1950s, telling of the joys and
sorrows, the triumphs and tragedies of the
working boat people, relating a way of life
that is now gone forever. Meticulously
researched and told with warmth and
sympathy by a true canal enthusiast.*
www.sgmpublishing.co.uk

Starlight *is a poignant tale of schoolboy friendship and loyalty, set alongside the Oxford Canal in 1955. It tells of one boy's discovery of the world of the waterways with his new friend, the local lock-keeper's son.*

'A beautiful tale, beautifully told'

Geoffrey Lewis' *Jess Carter* *stories are delightful, historically truthful canal-set tales for the younger reader, aged from ten to around a hundred.*
Set on the unusual tanker narrowboats of Thomas Clayton Ltd, in the months immediately before World War II, they too paint a realistic picture of the lives of the boating people.
The first book tells of a journey with a horse-drawn boat to Ellemere Port in Cheshire; the second describes the adventures of Jess and Luke Kain as they bring their new motor-boat from Uxbridge to Birmingham.

Thunderchild

Geoffrey Lewis first venture into the world of children's fantasy writing. Owing more to J.R.R.Tolkien than it does to J.K.Rowling, it is a thrilling tale of good against evil, of a young boy's discovery of his dormant powers as he takes up the task left to him by his dead father, to seek out and defeat the evil of Yorva, the Black Queen, in a world of magic and 'mythical' creatures.

Two more volumes are planned, making up the 'Lord of the Storm' Trilogy.

www.sgmpublishing.co.uk

Also by Geoffrey Lewis, the D.I. David Russell crime novels:

Published between 2003 and 2005, these four books relate David Russell's murder enquiries. The first book, Cycle, brings Russell and his regular side-kick, D.S. Doug Rimmer, together for the first time, and the other three titles tell of their ongoing partnership.

Some of these stories delve into the deepest, darkest corners of the human soul – but they also reflect the inherent, often unintentional, humour of human relationships. And there is light at the end of every tunnel, however long.

www.sgmpublishing.co.uk